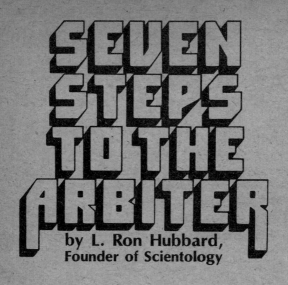

SEVEN STEPS TO THE ARBITER

by L. Ron Hubbard,
Founder of Scientology

MAJOR BOOKS • CHATSWORTH, CALIFORNIA

A MAJOR BOOKS FIRST EDITION

"SEVEN STEPS TO THE ARBITER"
was originally published as "THE KINGSLAYER"
copyright 1949 by Fantasy Publishing Co., Inc.

"THE BEAST" and "THE INVADERS"
copyright 1942 by Street & Smith Publications, Inc.,
renewed copyright © 1970 by Conde Nast Publications, Inc.

Copyright © 1975
by
MAJOR BOOKS
21322 Lassen Street
Chatsworth, California 91311

Published by arrangement with the author's agent,
Forrest J Ackerman, 2495 Glendower Avenue, Hollywood, CA 90027.

PRINTED IN THE UNITED STATES OF AMERICA

ISBN 0-89041-018-6

Library of Congress Catalog
Number: 75-13442

CONTENTS

Preface 7

The Kingslayer 8

The Beast 125

The Invaders 149

Preface

In 3922 the anarchy of governments in space was ended by mutual consent with the investment of enormous powers in the Galactic Arbitration Council. Heading this was the Arbiter who came to hold a position of absolute authority throughout known space.

The Arbiter with his council regulated and validated all currency. He passed upon the release and use of all weapons. His spies and emissaries were everywhere and presidents, kings and emperors bowed down.

The curtain of secrecy was drawn about all operations of the Council. Not one man in a thousand had ever heard of the Arbiter. Governments and great companies alone knew, for these depended for their very existence upon the Arbiter's permission.

But man is frail and space is large.

By 3975 the concerns of space were well awry and there were those who whispered. . . .

Chapter One

CHRISTOPHER RANDOLPH KELLAN KNEW HE had been born under an evil star. Not that he minded so much and not that it affected his merry grin. But it gave pain to many of his fellows.

He was a man with a temporary student pass. Beyond that he had no passport. He knew nothing of his mother or father and so might have had a difficult time proving he had been born, for he knew not where. And things happened to him, strange things which he could not explain except by believing in his evil star.

He was here today in the office of the Dean of Engineering of Terra University to account for himself again. He had been pugnacious. He had refused to believe. His professors did not like him because he thought too much and thought too well.

He stepped to the reception desk and the girl

there suddenly took his mind from his griefs. It was like forging through the desert cactus and finding a fountain with flowers growing 'round.

Her hair was jet and her tunic and lips were wine. And that was the downfall of Christopher Randolph Kellan. She seemed very struck by him. For his hair was gold, his shoulders broad. And they stood there for a space of thirty seconds—a very long time—looking, warm smiles growing between them.

And then she asked his name.

"Christopher Randolph Kellan," he answered. And her eyes flicked and fell. There was disappointment in her.

"They are waiting," she said.

"Just a minute. You're new here," said Kit. "I've been on the carpet thirty times and I've never seen you before. What's your name?"

His smile was engaging. He did not look like a man about to be hanged.

"They are waiting," she said coldly.

Christopher Randolph Kellan entered and stopped dead. He knew he was getting on their nerves but he had not expected the entire staff to congregate and tell him so. Yet in this shoddy old tomb of an office five members of the faculty sat, sad about the board, sadder when they saw Kit.

Dean Lapham anticipated the young man's move toward a chair. "You will stand, Kellan." And Kit looked at five pairs of heavy-lensed eyes upon him and not a smile in the crowd. A shuffle of feet behind him made him start.

The sixth man was sitting in the corner. He

was well dressed and so not of the university staff. His features were oddly brutal and with a chill Kit recognized in him the typical S.B.I. operative.

"This the fellow?" said the System Bureau of Investigation agent.

Dean Lapham, bald and grey about the shine, grey-coated and carpet slippered, looked very severely at Kit as though to make certain of the fact. He nodded politely to the S.B.I. man.

A small, dwarfish professor spread a tall pile of papers out before him and ruffled them with importance. He cleared his throat loudly to make up for his lack of size. "Christopher Randolph Kellan?" he queried. His voice broke at his effort of aggressiveness.

Kit caught a smile just in time and looked serious. "Yes sir."

"Kellan," said the dwarfish one, "I have your grades and attendance records here. Unless you can very well account for your conduct and this state of affairs something dire may happen to you."

The culprit was well aware of it. And he was well aware that no one present wanted the state of things accounted for.

"How old are you?" piped the dwarf.

"Thirty," said Kit.

The five heads inclined together. "Young," they agreed. "Very young to be taking his second master's degree."

"How long have you been at Terra University?" said Dean Lapham.

"One year," said Kit. He didn't like the way the S.B.I. man shuffled his feet each time he

10

spoke. He felt pounced upon.

They buzzed again. It was a sort of a court-martial, thought Kit, except that he didn't have his own counsel. He glanced behind him and saw that S.B.I. was still in his chair.

"From which school did you receive your master of theoretical engineering philosophy?" said Lapham.

"College of Nuclear Physics, Martian University," said Kit.

"Hmm," said Lapham. "You are certain."

"Of course I am. My sheepskin was stolen but Mars should be able to send the record."

"We have heard from Mars," said the dwarf, pulling out a light-thin letter. "They state that whereas you may have been a student there, no record is available in their files."

Kit started to speak hotly and then snatched at his temper and controlled it. He had argued once too often, that was why he was here.

"You finished high school right here in Washington, D.C.," said the dwarf, "but we have no further record. In 3960 you were given high school examinations at Woodwarde Prep of this city and passed them it says with honors. But you did not attend that school."

"I. . . . My Aunt Isabel had me taught by tutors until then. I lived here in the city."

"Who is this Aunt Isabel?" said Lapham.

"She is my aunt, my only living relative, sir. She is like my mother. When I am on Earth I live with her."

"Hah!" said S.B.I. He'd gotten something out of that but he subsided under the press of new questions from the faculty.

"You claim to have attended junior college at Vega's Demara in the city of Clarkville," said the dwarf, "and you gave us Thorpe College, Gamma Centauri's Bonner, City of Ghent for your basic engineering degree. Mr. Kellan," and his squeaky voice rose and broke with severity. "They have no record of your attendance at any one of these places despite the records you furnished us."

Now Kit was an amiable young man but he had red hair and red hair can stand just so many impossibilities. How could they have lost his records in every school? He clenched his fists. "Somebody," he said, "isn't telling the truth."

"Tut, tut, Kellan," said Lapham. "Bluster won't serve you here. Your transcripts are obviously false. Further, they show precocity enough to leave a blank of several years unaccounted for in your life. Where were you, for instance, two years ago?"

"I was a space sailor."

"What?" cried Lapham. "An engineering major a common sailor? How is this?"

"I liked it," said Kit stubbornly. "I've gone to school and then my Aunt has let me go where I pleased. I am a space navigator and have my papers from the Aldeberan Bureau of Space Inspection and Navigation. I suppose they are false as well. I am registered as a tubeman first class with your Earth Space Merchant Bureau. I do not see what this has to do with my scholastic standing! Somebody has stolen my papers from those places or somebody here is lying."

12

Lapham was going to batter him down but desisted. "Read on," he said to the dwarf.

"He is failing," said the dwarf, eyes a little shifty about it. "In binomial quadratics he received the grade of E. In his advanced spherical differentials he has just been conditioned. In the calculus of the tera-dimension he did not even attend his lectures. He demonstrated in an examination that he did not know the ten place logarithm table by heart."

"That will do," said Lapham. "Kellan, is it true that you have a bad habit of contradicting your professors and refusing to believe everything you are told?"

"I . . . they say so, sir."

"Is it true that you have made two original hypotheses in the field of matter creation?" said Lapham severely.

"I. . . ."

"No alibis, sir."

"I did," said Kit, unhappily.

"Did you or did you not state to Professor Hortle on my left that psychiatry was an infant science and beneath the notice of an engineer because we rely on experiments with rats and that human beings are not rats?"

"I . . . I did, sir."

"You attempted," said Lapham, "a short method of low order fission in the laboratory, did you not?"

"I . . . yes, sir," said Kit, acutely aware of the S.B.I. man's restlessness.

"You have corrupted students with free thought," said Lapham, scowling. "Have you not?"

"I have . . . I cannot help but state my ideas, sir."

"Ah!" said Lapham in triumph. "Then you confess to original thought!"

Kit flushed to the roots of his gold hair.

"You knew, of course," said Lapham, "that in an American University, all original thought is prohibited. That the deepest crime you can commit in this institution is refusal to believe and do and think exactly what you are told. You knew this!" Lapham turned to the others. "Gentlemen, he condemns himself. Shall we vote?"

They voted with an emphatic nod and turned as one to glare at Kit. Dean Lapham stood.

"Christopher Randolph Kellan," he said, "you are hereby expelled from the Terra University. I demand of you your student cards."

Kit started to give them up and then real fear struck him. Without a student card he could not eat, he could not work. They would give him back a yellow ticket which would make him shunned in any honest organization.

"You're condemning me to God knows what!" said Kit. "Your charges are false, they must be false. And as for thinking my own thoughts, originating new theories and concepts, when a man gets into the outposts of space your text books aren't worth firewood. I came here to learn more about being an engineer and I find you don't know enough to teach a straw boss how to push a wheelbarrow! Here's your cards and be damned to you!"

He tore them twice across and flung them on the floor.

14

A strong hand closed on his arm and whirled him.

"Come along, sonny," said S.B.I., "We got a place for you." Kit jerked free.

"Let's have your passport, sonny. I want to look at it."

Kit reluctantly gave him the passport. S.B.I. took it and looked at it closely. Then he pulled a bulky report from his coat and peered at it and so back to the passport.

"Your father and mother are dead," said S.B.I. smoothly. "Been dead since you were one year old. Where did they die?"

"Here in Washington, D.C.," bridled Kit.

"Vital statistics has disclosed that no one by that name died in the entire system in 3946. How do we account for that, sonny?"

"You can't. . . . It isn't true . . . they. . . ." But his mind whirled back. What did he know of them besides the name. Nothing. Even his Aunt Isabel had something mysterious about her, appearing and disappearing at intervals, having no friends, giving no parties. . . . Sometimes she would sit and cry for no reason and tell Kit he was a poor child and that he deserved better and she would cry again. He had always mistrusted himself in this. What did he know of his parents or even his nationality? It had all come up before, but not so seriously. He had not been a theoretical philosopher in engineering then, but just a college kid, doing a workaway on the space ships for the devil of it.

"No answer, huh?" said the S.B.I. "Don't know or won't tell. How is it a man as educated as you and with the experience you have floats into Terra University for a second master's degree, all his transcripts and his passport false? Why would he do it? I'll let you guess that, sonny, because you already know. Maybe you're not Kellan at all, but some other name, some other nationality."

"What do you mean to do?" asked the angry Kit.

"Why, to keep a trained engineer, who could wreck the system with the knowledge he's got from trying to wreck the system, of course. It's all under the head of security, sonny, and the place we got is plenty secure!"

"Give me my passport!"

"Why, sonny? You aren't going any place. Now get along!"

Chapter Two

WINE TUNIC AND JET BLACK DID NOT LOOK up when the two went out. She was studious in her regard for her shorthand notes. Kit looked back at her with regret and the S.B.I. gave him a healthy shove.

Impelled to the gravel walk not entirely in control of his way, Kit slammed into a dapper, spare gentleman who was evidently just entering. The gentleman reeled. Kit caught a hasty balance and apologized. But the dapper one had no smile for Kit.

"Well, well," he said to the S.B.I. "Another student in the toils of the law. Glad to see you fellows are on the job, officer. There's no telling what would happen in the system without you."

The S.B.I. said something idiotic about doing his duty and then snapped at Kit, "Why don't you look where you're going? Come now!"

"I say," said the dapper one, "if you haven't a car, I'll gladly have my chauffeur run down. Might come along myself and see the fun. Make a priceless story to tell Senator Maklin tonight. The other day he was saying some evil things about you chaps."

"It'd be putting you out," said the S.B.I.

"Not a bit, not a bit. Henry! Take this gentleman where he wants to go."

The car was a heavy black one with a ground license. It sidled up and Henry, a huge Negro of no expression whatever, stepped out to let the door open. S.B.I. saw the fancy interior complete with bed and bar and was a little awed. But he shoved Kit inside and then started to get in himself.

What happened then was a little bit confusing to Kit.

There was a dull pop and the S.B.I. man slumped forward like a dead man. The dapper one hadn't entered the building at all. He had come up behind S.B.I., drawn a wicked little gun and shot straight into the copper's spine. The big Negro changed expression not a whit. He picked up S.B.I.'s feet and got them inside so that the door would close. Then he went around, inverted the license, came back and stepped on the starter. The car went up through eight traffic lanes like a skyscraper express elevator, switched into the Arlington high speed track and was lost completely to Washington.

The dapper little man took a long cigar out of his black coat, cut off the end with a silver knife and lit up from a diamond-studded lighter. He puffed deeply and settled back with every sign of contentment.

Kit was staring down at the S.B.I. man who lay so still on the floor.

"Bother you?" said the dapper man. "Well, don't let it throw you, my friend. I dare say you'll get used to this sort of thing before you're through. Henry, the young man needs a drink."

Henry set the car on auto and turned his seat around while earth, ten thousand feet down, crawled by at five hundred and eighty. Return lane traffic, slightly below, fascinated Kit. Nobody at this wheel! But he took the drink that Henry mixed and was quite amazed to see the big, good-natured grin on Henry's face.

"Young man," said Henry, "if you don't like that, tell me. If you like it two or three more, tell me. And if you like too many more, tell me and I can fix that too. But I will say, young man, that you were pretty nice and cool and that's a pleasure to find." He nodded for emphasis and went back to his driving.

"Is he dead?" said Kit, not drinking.

"Good heavens, I should hope so!" And the dapper man looked closely at the corpse. "Frightened me there for a moment. Had to kill him, you know. Frightful things, disguises. Sticky. Changing car color, plates, chauffeur . . . messy, what? Much simpler this way. Oh, I say now. You object!"

"Well, yes," said Kit, "as a matter of fact, I do. A few minutes ago I was just an expelled student, my only crime was knowing too much and maybe thinking too hard about it. Now I'm an accessory to the fact of murder. Further, I suppose that you are a revolutionary agent bent on overthrowing the Terra System—down with Democracy, down with the United Planets of Sun. . . . Well? Aren't you?"

"My dear boy," said the dapper man, knocking the ashes from his cigar in a gesture of extravagance, "you pay me no compliment. Indeed no."

Kit scratched his gold hair and looked at the dead man. Kit's nose was stubbed, and wrinkled when he was worried. "I haven't called you a renegade. . . . Oh! Perhaps you belong to a group that wants to undermine the Six Nations, or . . ."

"Ah, yes. Terra, Centauri, Vega, Sirius, Procyon and Aldeberan. Henry! I say, how's that. Remember every single one of the six nations. My, my," he sank back and wreathed a grin. "Haven't thought of it since I was a boy in grammar school."

Kit felt offended. "Then I'm wrong. Excuse my unseemly curiosity. It's only that one usually likes to know the cause he is serving. Helps."

The dapper one put down the cigar in the tray. He took a lap robe and threw it over the dead man. Then, shooting his cuffs and straightening his tie-pin he stiffened into dignity.

"I have offended you," he apologized. "Let me introduce myself. I am Peter Vanpoll. My confederate at the wheel is Henry Mikmann. You have not been kidnapped but only rescued since it isn't clever of a country to run out its original thoughts, no matter the interests of security. I am just as much a friend of Terra and the government of Terra as your Dean Lapham or this S.B.I. man—probably more. Now, then." And he sank back and resumed his cigar.

This was all so much more confusion to Kit. "Sir, I know I am young. I know I did not even finish college. I have been told time and again that I am very stupid. But you have riddled me half to death. Here's a dead agent of the Terra government and yet you are a friend. . . ."

"A friend," said Peter Vanpoll, "but not a member. My young friend, have you any idea at all of the situation throughout the galaxy?"

"All I know is what I read in the newspapers," said Kit.

"Then you must confess your ignorance. Mr. Kellan. . . ." Kit started to realize that Vanpoll knew his name, ". . . how long has it been since the Six Planets fought amongst themselves?"

"Oh, about five hundred years."

"Good. How long has it been since the Twin Empires threatened war against Mother Terra?"

Kit scratched his gold hair. "About two hundred and fifty, more or less. But that's all ancient history. My golly, I had an ancestor that fought in it and I don't even know how many times great he was my grandfather. Twelve at least. What's that got to do . . . ?"

"Now there are about six thousand planets in space, constituting some twenty-seven leagued combines of systems," said Peter Vanpoll. "There are eight major empires with the remainder acting as extra territory or tribute systems or combinations of systems. Am I right?"

"I suppose so," said Kit dubiously. He had always flunked history.

"Well now, that's the size of it," said Peter Vanpoll. "Eight major empires. Terra, controlling the Six Nations and the Twin Empires, so-called, is the mother. But the eight have forgotten sentiment. With the chatter about inter-galactic flight—through lord knows where these crackpots get such insane ideas. . . ."

"Inter-stellar flight was supposed to be impossible fifteen hundred or two thousand years ago," disagreed Kit.

"Was it? Well, I daresay you're better at history than I. Anyway, with threatened intergalactic flight and all the attendant monkeybusiness, it's obvious that eight empires and their satellites are too many. The Marco-Trigon War of last year was not decisive. But there will be another war and another and another. Silly, but there will. Our galaxy is too crowded. People are starving throughout the systems. And people are scared. . . ."

"I don't see what this has to do with a dead S.B.I. man," said Kit.

"Well, let it go. There's one man and one council that guides the unrest, that profits from this galaxy's uncertain political future. One man and one council loans the money, gets the profit, chooses the rulers, starts the wars. . . ."

22

He was saying it as casually as "Nice kitty, pretty kitty," and his audience didn't quite get a start on it. Suddenly Kit looked round-eyed as though Peter Vanpoll had left his senses.

"The Arbiter!" said Kit. And he quickly took a drink.

"Hah!" said Peter Vanpoll. "We aren't so dull or so poorly read as we pretend. It's supposed to be mutiny to say that. And yet Earth arms to her toes in case the balance goes wrong and while she arms and amends the United Planet constitution and spends public works money for new battleships, she runs deep into debt with the Arbiter. . . ."

"The Galactic Arbitration Council," said Kit and took another quick drink.

"Precisely. Well, there you have it my boy. The Arbiter and his lads keep everybody spending to fight and collect the interest and promote a war now and then and there you are. Ah, yes, there you are."

He seemed to have forgotten there was more to the subject for he puffed a long time on his cigar and pointed out the beauty of the sunset.

"See here," said Kit. "We're on dangerous ground. It is said that the Arbiter has paid spies everywhere, even in the governments. It's said that all security is just a mask to keep the Arbiter informed. If this is a trap to lead me into dangerous statements. . . . Just who are you?"

Peter Vanpoll smiled a placid smile and relighted his cigar. "Me?" he said. "Why, nothing's simpler, lad. I'm agente for this galactic quadrant of the People's Revolutionary Society.

And I've just rescued a charming young man with too much wit for his own good and I am taking him to Terra headquarters where I hope to persuade him to join us."

"Join what? To do what?"

"Join the P.R.S., of course."

"All right. But what would I do?"

"Mr. Kellan, you have a brilliant mind. Its sins are originality and versatility. Your memory is not good and memory is the educational gauge of your country. But you've an inquiring head and you've a taste of original construction. I'm backing you."

"To do what?" insisted Kit.

"You see nations entangled in wars. You see people starving, treasuries in debt, taxes out of sight. You see ruin on every hand. Would you like to make your people and the people of space free? Of course you would. Any thinking young man with an ounce of patriotism would. So join us."

Kit was patient. "To do what, Mr. Vanpoll?"

"Why, as to that you see, we've a corps of picked young men who are trained and dedicated to just one thing: the killing of the Arbiter."

"The kil. . . . Say now. Wait! Nobody even knows who he is nor where. . . ."

"Well, that's the job ahead. Now I'll not persuade you against your will. Save your country, save space and the galaxy or. . . ."

"Or what?"

"Why, then Henry and I will have to go back and dump you in a Washington city park with this body and the gun and let you go your happy way."

"No!"

"Ah, then," said Peter Vanpoll. "I see you have decided to join. Henry, isn't that Cuba over there? I think we're about home."

Chapter Three

HE SUPPOSED THE DRINK MUST HAVE BEEN drugged for when he woke he had no connective recollection of entering the house and going to bed and to sleep. He last recalled spiraling down upon a coral driveway amid banana plants and palms. And now he was awakening in a soft bed and a soothing Caribbean breeze was softly playing with the big wooden shutters at his window. Grass mats were on the floor and a few lazy lizards about two inches long were on the white walls but the furniture was very old, very massive, very beautiful. A banana plant patted dreamily against the unglassed sill of the casement and waves were whispering just outside.

Christopher Randolph Kellan sat up. No headache. He looked at his pajamas and found them to be silk. And then there was a silvery clink of dishes and somebody was right beside him. He jumped.

A beaming Chinese put the tray in place but he was no servant. He was wearing a loose jacket and a small hand gun plainly showed under his armpit.

"Come on now and eat like a good fellow," said the Chinese. "Make you feel better. Henry always puts too much in those drinks. He's a big man and his tissue absorption gives him radical notions of how much the average body can stand. I always make it about half one of his doses. Of course you're a pretty big man yourself and maybe he knew what he was doing. Now eat up because the secretary is coming in a couple minutes and you won't get a chance."

Without waiting for any comment the talkative Oriental withdrew and sat down in a chair outside the door, tilting it back against the wall and pulling out a "British Sporting Journal" to which he pleasantly applied himself.

Kit was not used to such service. A student mess hall had been lacking on silver. His breakfast sparkled and he tasted it, found it good and was about to get down to it in earnest when a little man came in with a huge briefcase and an arm load of papers which kept sliding to the floor. From his pocket he pulled a pen and an ancient bottle of ink, looked around in perplexity and then set it down amid the breakfast. This triumph cheered him and he nodded very happily at Kit.

Papers waterfalled over the bed, leaped from the briefcase and the little man's pockets and joined the crowd. Then pen alert and form on knee, the little man squirmed comfortably down in the bedside chair and said rapidly: "Name age, address (that will be here), next of kin (in case of burial, you know), father's name, mother's name, father's business (but we can do without that), hobbies. . . ."

Kit gagged on a mouthful of toast. "Wait a minute!" he wailed. "I can't begin to answer half of that."

The little man looked pained. "The forms, you know. I must fill the forms. What if we had to ship the remains and had no address? What then? Huh, I imagine you'll have a hard time getting around that, now."

"I am Christopher Randolph Kellan. I am an orphan since birth. I have no idea what my father did. I have an aunt, Isabel Crane, who gave me my early home. I was educated in a private school, grammar school and high school. . . ."

"Hah! Then nobody will be much disturbed about the remains. Fine, fine. No other relatives?"

"No. My aunt really isn't my aunt either. She was my mother's best friend. I know nothing of my family. Now fill them in any way you like and if it's the same to you, I'm hungry."

"Oh, I wouldn't dream of disturbing your breakfast. Go right on eating and don't mind me. Now just why," he said, scribbling with the scratchy pen and getting ink on his nose in some unaccountable fashion, "did you decide to dedicate your heart and body to the slaying of the Arbiter?"

Kit looked at the remorseless fellow and sighed as he looked mournfully at the plate of scrambled eggs. "I didn't decide anything. I was kidnapped and you know it."

"Hah! Then you think the Arbiter is a fine person?"

"I don't. I know that somebody manipulates the strings and that empires fall or rise, crops fail, wars happen, plague spreads. . . . Peter Vanpoll says it's the Arbiter. Okay, let it ride. I'm just a boy from Earth. . . ."

The little man's pen was flying and then he looked up and pinned Kit with a cunning glare. "You never followed curriculum in school. You read everything you could find and your private tutors let you in spite of the law. Now, isn't that right?"

"Yes," said Kit, mouth full of eggs.

"They all say it!" crowed the little man. "They read forbidden books and do forbidden experiments and they wind up here. Every time. They all give the same answer. Hee, hee! What fine revolutionary stock. Finest minds in the business. Inquiring. . . . What are your ideas about love?"

Now if another thing had not happened just then, Kit would have said so truly that women were just women. But wine and jet, no less, at that moment came in with a bunch of flowers, nodded to him with a smile and put the fragrant blooms on the chest by the window. She sat down on the sill and looked out upon the cheerful day.

There was sunlight in her and the curves were so remarkable under that white silk tunic that Kit opened and closed his mouth several times in the fond belief that he was speaking.

"What," insisted the little man severely, "are your ideas about love? Women, I must warn you, can be very dangerous to such a mission as you are attempting. The Arbiter controls everything, has spies everywhere and many of those spies are women. Women are very useful procuresses of information. Now, what are your ideas about love?"

"Wonderful," whispered Kit at last.

"What?" cried the little man.

"Wonderful," sighed Kit.

"He means me, professor," said jet and wine.

The little man whirled about and was about to reprove her. But the radiance of her youth unmanned him. He gave her a sickly smile. "My questions are only the standard ones, dear."

"Keep your eyes on the room side of my tunic," said jet and wine.

The little man flushed. "I beg pardon, my dear. As soon as I finish with this boy. . . ."

"He's no boy," said jet and wine, crossing to the stricken Kit. "He's a very fine young man and I think he has a very interesting face. Don't you, Christopher Randolph Kellan?"

"My dear girl," said the little man, "my interrogation. . . ."

"Bah," said jet and wine. "I gave it all to you from the university records. Now fly away like a good little man and don't hurry back."

The scribe got up, papers and quill a massive problem as he struggled to put them away. "You've no right here, you know. When Peter comes and finds you've been talking to our pris . . . to the guest, he won't be pleased."

"Fie on Peter. He's such a jealous dear. Now go 'way."

Stubbornly the little man tried to stand his ground but beauty conquered him and he shuffled to the door. "You should not have permitted her to come in," he complained to the Chinese sentry.

"You shouldn't permit her to drive you out," said the sentry with a grin and promptly went back to working out the speeds of various horses in the last derby.

The little man was still retreating, but he flung a last shot. "You leave this afternoon on your first job, Kellan. So be very sure you are ready."

This shook Kit out of his rapt gazing. "Wait! Hey you. Wait a minute! What first job? I. . . ."

The door slammed on the retreat. Kit looked at jet and wine.

"I'm Carla," she said, perching herself on the bed and helping herself to his toast and coffee. "They all talk like they own me but I'm nobody's girl. Not yet. I pick and choose as fancy suits me and so it's never suited me yet. I'm twenty-six, a master of sabotage, a member of the P.R.S. in good standing and I earn my pay. My people are dead, I have nineteen thousand dollars saved up, I'm chaste and pure, I can cook and sew and fly a car, and I've been your girl since yesterday afternoon. Now you tell me about yourself."

"Why there's nothing much. . . . What did you say?"

"I said I've been your girl since yesterday afternoon. You're cute, as they say in the love story magazines. What dye do you use on your hair? Oxblood shoe polish?"

Kit poured himself a cup of coffee. He had not yet assembled his wits. Then he succeeded. He put the cup down untasted, he took her right hand and pulled it toward him and then he kissed her.

It shocked them both as though they had contacted high voltage with their lips, for all that she had been playing jokes on him and for all that his kiss was half punishment. They fell apart and sat staring at each other.

"It . . . it's Kit, isn't it?" she said.

"Carla."

She stood up and did a dance step and then sat down again. She looked at him more closely and was leaning toward him when she abruptly changed her mind. She stood up.

"Well, well," she said, "I'll bet you're wondering how I got into the dean's office. I was proud of that. His girl got sick and her room mate should have reported for work but then she had an accident and lost all her passports, poor dear. And I suppose you are wondering just why you were expelled so suddenly and without warning. I heard it directly from the dean. You broke a law." She tried to think of it and then perked. "The Law of Conservation of Energy. Did you waste some energy, Kit?"

He noted that her voice trembled a little. But he was too taken by storm not to be grateful for the respite. "That's no real law, silly. It's a law in basic physics and anybody can break it. You simply work out the Durak's formula so that output over input is bigger than one. . . ."

"La! Sir Engineer, I've nothing in my head but sawdust, she smiled prettily," said Carla. "In my own little inimitable way I am what the common herd calls a wowzer, but engineering. Well, but there you are. You are a theoretical engineering philosopher, it said in the records, and look where it got you."

"Yes," said Kit, sobering and looking around him. Then he remembered. "They said I was to go on a job. Does that mean I just sail off and shoot somebody or what?"

"Oh dear no. It's not to be that simple . . ." and then she masked her eyes, growing cold to him. "Isn't the breeze nice. It's been so hot lately."

Kit regarded her for a little and drank the coffee.

"Two or three thousand years ago they had pirates around here," she said. "They made you walk the plank and took your doubloons, whatever those are. Sounds indecent, doesn't it?"

Kit looked at her over his cup.

"And here we sit," she said, "two thousand years later as pretty a gang of cutthroats as ever ran up a Jolly Roger. That's pirate for flag," she explained.

Kit looked very steadily.

She got up. "No. I won't tell you. There are things you have to find out for yourself."

"How many in this corps of assassins?" said Kit.

"As if I knew!"

Now one of the most prominent personal characteristics about Kit was that he was nobody's fool. Impetuous, sometimes indiscreet, always too honest intellectually, he had something besides a good smile and a gift of blarney. He could tell when people were sad or happy or well or sick by some sort of eighth sense. He could also tell when they were lying.

"A thousand?" he said.

"Heavens no!"

"Just a couple dozen?"

"Kit, you be quiet. You are trying to make me betray my sworn cause. My ideals. My very soul writhes. . . ."

"Where do I locate the Arbiter and what is he?"

"As to that, who knows? As to what he is, he's the power behind the throne, the fist in every bank, the maker of laws."

"How'd it happen?"

"Why, somebody a long time ago got the idea it would be wonderful, seeing that wars were so dangerous, to establish a Council to arbitrate all disputes among governments. So they set up a great affair. And then somebody said it was money, not soldiers that made for power and they gave the Council a bank, every government contributing so much. And so things went along fine until the present day."

"What happened?"

"How do I know? All I can tell you is that it will be a fine thing when the Arbiter is killed."

Now just why he could not say but Kit felt she was lying. Maybe her facts were limited.

"Oh bother all that," said Carla. "Kit, I am worried. Here I've just fallen in love with you and off you go. Maybe they'll kill you. Maybe they'll get you to make up some unholy weapon to kill the Arbiter's men and you'll blow yourself up with it. Maybe. . . ." She had started with enough bravado, she thought, to carry her.

But Kit saw that the tears trembling on her lids were quite honest. "Come here!" he said.

She stepped nearer. He grabbed her and was just starting to kiss her.

"Oh, really now," said Vanpoll in the door. "I say, but that's a trifle thick, what?"

He was carrying a suitcase in one hand and an envelope in the other; suitcase, envelope and Vanpoll all sagged.

Carla came up in confusion and rushed to the door. She recalled herself when she had passed Vanpoll and waved back. "Good-bye, Kit. Good-bye and remember me!"

Vanpoll shut the door and Kit, coming back to this world, looked curiously at him. For Peter Vanpoll was trembling and his cheeks were blanched and there was a very studied atmosphere about him as he put down the suitcase.

"Here are your orders," said Vanpoll, coolly. "And here is a kit you'll need." He looked at the door, caught himself and unfastened the case.

Kit wanted to say he was sorry but he wasn't. "It was all right," he fumbled. "She was. . . ."

"My dear, dear fellow, you have a great deal

to learn. Probably your first lesson here should be that your mission is far too dangerous—" and Kit thought the man relished that word vengefully,—"far too dangerous to admit toying about with women."

"Sir," began Kit hotly.

"No, no. My apologies. Carla is no ordinary woman. Nor is she my girl nor anyone's girl. It appeared to me this morning when she arrived that she was preoccupied, and when I teased her about it she became extremely angry. I should have known. But we aren't all lucky enough to have red hair, now, are we? But to business. Here is your gear."

A strange uniform came out. It was brilliant scarlet and was laced and trimmed with gold. A half-cape came from one shoulder and a glittering aiguillette with a diamond tip from the other. It was stiff with bullion and haughty with rank. Thigh-high space boots, sheening black with varnish were matched by a wide belt with a gold buckle from which was suspended a mimic spaceman's box good for nothing but tobacco. The entire uniform was refined down from high utility to gaudy display and was easily enough to blind a man—or more especially a woman. The helmet itself, solid gold over a fine undentable frame, was quite useful, having an atmosphere mask and cartridges, a small radio and a light projector worked into the mock ram's horns on each side.

Kit shaved and bathed while Vanpoll talked.

"They've a new wave source on Sun 12, Planet Ringo, Marcon Empire. That's ninety-seven light years from here," said Vanpoll. And then he began to give street names and people's names and threatened sudden death if Kit forgot.

While Kit dressed Vanpoll concluded, "This is the first step of seven steps to the Arbiter. Don't ask what next or why. Obtain the wave source from the commander of the technicians at Laboratory Zeta. All your credentials are in order. Henry will get you to Mars with your own ship so your departure won't be noticed."

Kit looked at his glittering self and marveled that he could get into it, so near was the perfect fit.

"Your are a special technician of the Greater Triad with the rank of Captain General. Regulations and particulars of that service will be found in your luggage which waits below. Study it well. Remember to speak nothing but pure Esperanto and none of your dialects. Remember what you know as a trained engineer and probably you'll get by."

"Why do you want the wave source?"

"Good-bye," said Vanpoll, coldly.

Chapter Four

THEY HAD HIM, KIT THOUGHT MOODILY. HE
was staring at a comet they were passing on
its own course and direction and experienced
nostalgia. As a boy he'd dreamed of being a
comet in the engineering world. Complete with
a fiery tail. And what had happened? He had
thought too much.

He'd studied hard and on his own. And then
he'd taken that trip to the Vega System on the
cattle freighter and he'd found out what it was
to be tough and to live hard. Those years had
unmanned him for a student. He'd bucked
roulette at Dinky's and drunk everybody under
the table and fought half the royal navy with
his bare fists. He'd been branded a hard case
even by a pirate captain who had then offered
him a job as mate. He'd deserted in Mangapoor
and for two months had shot tigers for the
farmers at fifty cents a tiger. He'd been a

bouncer in Toelin for three weeks in the toughest bottle joint on the Barcary Port. He'd shipped for South Gillipon as an assistant tubeman and had landed in that ice-choked land as first mate all by the dint of his fists. Didn't make a good student out of him when the university chance was thrown his way. He'd paid dear for that experience in the spaceways. His career.

The comet was dropping rapidly astern and the boot-licking top-port steward was nudging him with a tray of chocolate and buns. Kit came back to his universe. He smiled at the steward and the man bobbed happily. But Kit was smiling because the man didn't know that the braid to which he gave those bows had, just a year ago, been much lower than a steward on a space can, much less a crack liner.

"Beautiful view," said the steward. "There's a black nebula just ahead that I'm sure you'll enjoy, sir." And he bowed away from the deck chair.

Just a tourist, Kit told himself.

And then the gloom came back. Black nebula was a symbol for him now. He'd get shot at this business sure. But they had him and had him well. He'd no passport of his own, no cards to eat or work anywhere in all space and that left him only the pirates—and who'd die that swift death under a cruiser's soundless guns? Or in a crib with a mate's knife in your spine? Piracy was not morally wrong, it was merely dirty, scary sort of stuff where the tubes broke down and you didn't dare put in anywhere and you orbited forever around some dark star, a hundred men in a rusty tub. This way he at least had his passport.

Yes, he sighed, sinking back and stretching out his legs, there was Carla. And this he could think upon for hours. Hours and hours and space unit days. There were problems like, Had those been real tears? or, She couldn't have meant she really was his girl by her own choice . . . ?

"Frightful bore isn't it?" said a man in a nauseous tweed cap.

Kit started violently and arrested his hand halfway to his top pocket where the flat gun lay. And then, "I beg pardon."

"I say, it must be frightfully stupid to you military men, buzzing through all this emptiness. Been forward counting the meteorites we've picked up on the bow. Dreadful bore. Going to Sun-Twelve?"

"Probably stop there," hedged Kit. Safe answer. The *Presidential Herald* made no other stop going this way.

"Horrible place. Provincial, the whole system. Stupid sort of an empire anyway. Goats hold it together. Don't blink. It's the truth. Goats, goats, goats. Baaa baaa. Horrible place. Going to be there long?"

"Couldn't say. Schedules."

"Of course. Ghastly thing, schedules. Spend two days getting from one system to another and then five days trying to catch a shuttle ship from one broken down planet to the next. Old-fashioned equipment and all. Break downs. Did have a mutiny stop me once, though."

"Well, well," said Kit, who had participated

in two and been a ringleader in a third when the captain stopped all the water except to the cargo of pigs.

"Oh, yes. But it was quelled. Two chaps hung and it was quelled. They were going to sell all the passengers to the Arak slavers, or so the mate told us at dinner that night."

Knowing mates, Kit smiled.

"Well, it would have been quite an adventure. I say, permit me to introduce myself. I'll Morgan Carlyle, of Dombey and Dombey."

Kit expected him to say he sold lady's underwear and was therefore entirely amazed when the fellow added:

"We set up electrical equipment in test labs. They have some frightful new thing up on Ringo; that's the capital of the Marcon Empire."

Kit almost fell on his fellow-traveler's neck. Maybe he was only a couple of weeks from Carla!

"New wave Stuff?" said Kit.

"Yes, I seem to recall it as such. Awful bore, terrible equations. It selects one kind of rock from another, disintegrates either at desire. Revolutionize mining and building or some such thing. But you military men. . . ."

"Coincidence," beamed Kit at his most winning. "Coincidence indeed. I'm Tourney, special technician of the Greater Triad, on my way this very minute to inspect that equipment for war uses. Mr. Carlyle, I certainly am happy to meet you."

"Well, imagine that!" said Carlyle, picking up. "Coincidence indeed. Though confidentially, old fellow, I knew your insignia and guessed why you were going else I wouldn't have spoken so plainly. Security and all that. I'm to buy it for the Arbiter, you probably have already guessed. But you'll be one of his men. Greater Triad high command, eh?" and he nudged a knowing elbow into Kit's ribs.

"Ha, ha!" said Kit and managed a splendid wink.

"Ha, ha!" said Carlyle. "But really no coincidence at all. Just trying to draw you out, saw you on the passenger list this very morning. The Arbiter's agent said there'd be a Greater Triad man on the spot to see that we got all the proper data and no hold-out. So here we are, partners in crime, what?"

Kit tried not to look so suddenly pale. "Indeed so. Ha, ha! Partners in crime." But he knew he was going to feel most terribly unnerved the rest of the trip.

The Greater Triad man on the spot . . . ye Gods!

Were their firing squads painful on Ringo?

Chapter Five

CHRISTOPHER RANDOLPH KELLAN, CURRENT-
ly Captain General Tourney of the Triad Emperor's Technical Own, was at once happy and
unhappy to get to Ringo, home planet of the
Marcons. For one thing he had gotten, in the
past week, "most frightfully bored" with Morgan Carlyle's boredom. Pleading a weak stom-
ach but really to guard a tongue, Kit had refused to drink. He had, however, whiled away
a few hours each day playing chess for which
they each had something of a knack.

They stood on the landing tower, blocking
the egress of less important passengers, and
surveyed the city before climbing down.

"Frightfully boring place, what?" said
Carlyle.

Kit didn't think so. Ringo was a three-
quarter G carbon planet with eight climatic
zones, six seas and some ninety thousand foot

mountains which, snow-covered now, hung serenely above the lovely green plain where nestled Gloriana, the capital city of the whole empire. A wandering, shining river, the mountains and the polished red roofs of the alabaster city made this appear to be a green, white and scarlet setting and jewel in space's often rigorous or heroic ports.

As always, one envisioned a system as balls about a central sun until he started landing. Then he conceived himself as able to look at the whole planet in a glance. But finally, when ground was there, the buildings were taller than he and the trees higher and the horizon distant and one was then very solidly on and "in" a settlement. From a speck in the universe for the system, the passenger landed found a whole universe in a house before him.

They went down the tower and out the gate to the taxi line. There was a small fleet of blue and white cabs and a swarm of ordinary human beings scrambling for them, bright coats and flying luggage blending in swirl of colorful and noisy motion.

Buffeted about, Carlyle bleated, "Going to the local hostelry and fight their bedbugs. Coming?"

Kit didn't want to do any such thing but he hesitated as he groped for an alibi. It was the moment he spent standing there which brought him a new danger.

A tow-headed, grease stained, overalled fight-scarred quartermaster of an in-port tramp stopped dead, gaped and, every hair on end in amazement, walked straight up to Kit, .

44

peering in disbelief.

"It ain't . . . my gawd, it couldn't be . . . KIT!"

Black scarf, ragged spacecoat, rum stink and all it was Spica Mike McBain, far, far off his beat in the Six Nations. True to the old wheeze that you ain't never in foreign parts until you meet a spaceman friend from your own home town, Spica Mike made this a very foreign port.

Stiff with anxiety, Kit unwittingly made a very good picture of the officer outraged. Poor Spica Mike, how he'd have to cut him down. "My dear fellow," said Kit, "I am sure I have never had the pleasure."

The quartermaster gawped. Fast in action he was not too quick of wit. He continued to gawp until Kit almost wore out the right eye winking. Carlyle couldn't see that side.

"Kit, I. . . ."

Wink, wink, wink, wink, wink. "Really, how you could have the nerve to suppose I knew you." Wink, wink, wink, wink, wink. Wouldn't he ever understand?

Carlyle was looking very odd.

"If you ain't Kit Kellan . . ." began Spica Mike. And then the wink finally got to him. He fumbled and grew confused. "Gosh, I'm mighty sorry, sir. I knowed a bloke as like you as Gemini. Beggin' your pardon, sir. Don't have the cops on me. I'm just a poor space quartermaster and I ain't rightly got me blinkers what with age and rum."

And then Spica Mike added, stir fashion, the way they talk in the cells of Cerebos, "Pull the toff on me, willya. Meet me at Spaceman's Rest at nine, you toff."

And aloud, "Please don't have me arrested. I got wives and kids." And he backed away, that scrofulous old pirate that had maybe twenty wives and half a hundred kids on as many planets.

Kit, a little weak, got into the cab. "Intelligence work. Certainly associates one with the riff-raff."

Carlyle was narrow-eyed but held his peace. "The Royal Empire Hotel, driver. Unless you've another one in mind, general."

"Like to go past the royal palace?" said the driver. "They just got her painted blue and man, she's a sight to see. The princess was out riding to hounds this morning but I suppose it's too late to see her come back, though it's a treat, gentleman, I assure you."

"Blue, my God," groaned Carlyle. "The building is solid copper and they've painted it blue. These German princes! No taste. Frightful people."

It restored his good humor and he apparently had forgotten the incident at the cab line.

"Let's go by," said Kit, taking the bold course. "I want to present my credentials and have a look at the royal shops and labs this afternoon."

"Ah, certainly. By all means. The palace, driver."

Two hours later, heels sore with standing, back half sprained with bowing and knees dusty with kneeling, Kit and Carlyle came out of the palace. They sank at a table at a sidewalk cafe and Carlyle ordered cold wine.

"Be beastly but what can you expect in the provinces," said Carlyle. He sighed, depressed. "What terrible taste. Orange gown. Blue crown. Ghastly. Now tell me honestly, General, did you ever see the like of these dumpy German rulers out here. I swear, when he heard the Arbiter's name we were lucky he didn't try to sell us his sceptre. Probably had false rubies in it, though."

Kit was quiet as he drank. It gave him pause to see that his own bogus orders had not impressed the Emperor one single bit, Greater Triad or no Greater Triad. But the mention of the Arbiter and a little card that talked aloud which Carlyle had diffidently extended had all but given them the kingdom. And how the dumpy little monarch had squealed and quibbled about prices for the gadget his technicians had invented and how bored Carlyle had been. The Arbiter it seemed, bought at his own price.

But there was one relief in it. The real Greater Triad man had not yet presented his orders.

"Let's go to the labs," said Kit with sudden energy.

"Good Lord, what ambition. We can kill days at this and the next ship out won't go for a week."

"I'm going, then," said Kit.

"Then I suppose I must," said Carlyle, suddenly watchful.

They hailed a cab and were shortly being stopped by an enormous gate beyond which the vehicle could not continue. And they became very involved with captains of the guard and intelligence men of the empire. But soon they were allowed to continue through to the central laboratory where, amid whirring dynamos and huge piles of iridium wire their man sat.

He was a young man and he said his name was Joyce. He was very humble and had a pale, stooped way about him.

"It isn't very much," he said, "but I can't seem to get anyone here to understand it. They build what I tell them and all the plans have to stay here in my safe. They haven't let me leave the building for three months." He was plaintive, rather beaten down. No color to him. But when it came to technical knowledge, the man was an inspiration.

"I had to do it, you see, to get through the mountains. Aerial transmission is all right but have you ever tried to bring a cow to market in an airplane?"

Kit had but he let it go.

"And so," said the pale young man, amongst a thousand coils of wire, "we had to have a way to get through the mountains cheaply. And so I made a qualitative selector which disintegrates any required kind of rock. This, when focused upon and tuned to a vein of, say quartz, removes all the quartz up and down a forty-foot band—a thing which I can adjust. So, to go through a mountain all one does is find schist or a vein of quartz and start to go. It operates on frequency transmission. One rock acts differently . . . but then, you'd rather see it work, I suppose. Here is the model. The king said you were coming."

He had a section of mountain about forty meters square, a vein of quartz ten feet wide straight through it.

He picked up an electrode and drove it into the top of the quartz and he put a piece of quartz against the machine to get its wave action. Then he grounded the other end of his coils and set up a pair of inverted blowers.

"Dust, you know," he apologized. "Wouldn't want to get you dusty." The scarlet uniform really impressed him.

He threw a switch with, "Dear me, I hope it works," and the place was a bellow of sound and a hurricane of air.

The quartz vein vanished, leaving a polished sidewall in the country rock and a sharp pass ten feet high through the mock mountain.

He shut off the machine. "It worked," he said sadly. "But really, it's hard to make them. Nobody seems to understand the type of wave but myself and I've no mathematics to express it to them. Nobody here ever studied quad-dimensional calculus."

"I guess he has us there, eh?" said Carlyle.

But it didn't have Kit. He at once began to run through the system and nod his bright hair over it. He took a pencil from his breast pocket and started to make cryptograms on a coil box.

"You've one too many resistances. It will work faster with your eighteenth stage inverted and its amplitude increased. Further, according to this distintegration speed, if you mounted the thing on a force beam so—" and he drew rapidly on a piece of plywood scrap "—you could speed it up to about thirty miles an hour. How fast did you calculate it?"

"Allowing for the removal of debris," said the young man, eyes getting bright, "I had it at twenty. Say! That's right!" And he watched Kit who, with a slight smile, was making quad-dimensional calculus equations on the plywood. "That's right! Say! You molecularize the debris with a smaller disintegrator on each blower and float it all out as air! Thirty miles an hour! We could drill through mountains at fifty! Why we could fix a landscape full of roads and subways. . . ."

"Or mount it on a tank's nose," said Carlyle, getting the drift, "and attack through hitherto impassable ranges."

That damped them a little. For the moment Kit was in pure creation. But his flying pencil and hurriedly pointed weaknesses and strengths were a worshipful fascination to the pale young man. Carlyle, having followed but poorly, became bored.

"Come on up to the hotel and play a bit of chess," he said.

"So there you have your chance to explore the interiors of planets for the first time," said Kit to the pale young man. "Now what we need. . . ."

Carlyle watched. They were hauling out all manner of junk and knocking together from an old gun turret and some truck wheels a thing which looked like nothing Carlyle would ever want. Kit's uniform was getting stained and rumpled and the pale young man was flushed with excitement.

By six o'clock Kit was stripped to the waist,

his splendid torso agleam with sweat, his gold hair burning like a torch and his eyes bright with inspiration through the mask of grease. The pale young man, infected, tousled and fatigued, stood back to admire their queer contraption.

"It's very like a tank I saw in an ancient history," said the pale young man. "And all it needs is a good, strong fault to chew its way to the very bowels of Ringo. General, I honor you. My concourse with high brass until now made me feel distinctly that they could not sweat nor stink of axle grease. Do you think it will work?"

"My dear fellow," said Carlyle, "what with being blinded by your adhesion torches and deafened by your blows and language, I cannot give you any kind of judgment. But if crudity and lack of smooth design means anything at all, the first man who tries that thing will surely but succeed in digging himself a very deep and proper grave. What a bore. Come, Tourney old chap. A bath will do much to cool the fires of your inspiration and make the smell of you more companionable. It's a fine thing you don't play chess as well as you enthuse with machinery or else I'd be poorer by ten thousand dollars now. Come before I swoon of ennui and hunger."

"Leave it right there," said Kit, "and let it champ for action as it will while you scout out a vein of fine chewing rock. Maybe we can test it this very night."

"Scientizing is confoundedly like prison to me," said the pale young man, indignant for the first time as he thought of it. "They'll not even let me out in the yard. I'm to be sold like a text on bat raising or a set of wrenches and they keep me near. I'm worth they tell me at least four million to the crown and that's the pay for the emperor's sister's wedding. To think my genius goes to prepare a nupital bed for two German clowns who couldn't mend a hairpin were it bent! Tell me, am I to be kept thus when I'm bought for this thing in my head?"

"Daresay," said Carlyle, yawning.

"There may be some escape," said Kit and then, without Carlyle seeing, he gave the lad a most confidential wink. "But just now look up that vein of rock."

"But the guards and the intelligence men. I'm worth four million boxed up here."

"We'll ask for very special permission and you'll be allowed the yard. Mind, I may see you tonight at nine or ten or eleven for I may think of some improvement. You might try digging a bit with it outside and if it works, we're that much ahead."

"Oh I will, I will," said the young man, not so pale, seeing a second wink. There was that in his voice which promised Kit he had gained a faithful and enduring following of one engineer.

"See you later," said Kit.

At the gate, still struggling into his skin-clinging jacket and belt, Kit told the intelligence men there was a test in progress and they looked at his epaulets and overlooked his grease and bowed deferentially, promising faithfully to let the young man out of his prison and aid in removing the machine to the yard.

At the hotel Carlyle watched Kit bathe while dinner was on its elegant way to their suite. "You have a taste for work that's queer in your rank, old boy. The Arbiter merely wanted the man and the formulas and you've knocked together a new machine. Exhausting, if I may say so. Always considered cogs and rods as frightful bores. Well, here's dinner."

Kit, dressed again, sat down to the crystal and gold plate, indolent in appearance but with one eye solidly on the clock. If the gods were good he'd be out of here before the real general showed up. Nine o'clock.

Chapter Six

KIT LET THE GAME DRAG UNTIL THE CLOCK
said eight-thirty. He had never played half out
for Carlyle, it being very fine policy to let a
man you can use win at least half of the time.
And so Carlyle went on long excursions with
bishops and knights, got out of traps that
didn't close, six times couldn't see how his
attempted checkmates came so near and yet
were so far and withdrew to puzzle more.

At eight-forty, Kit made a sudden sortie
with his queen and gobbled up a rook. It caught
Carlyle's king on his own square, uncastled.
That was check. Carlyle interposed his queen.
Kit backed his queen with a bishop. Carlyle in
panic tried to get a knight into play and then
it happened with terrible suddenness. Kit took
Carlyle's queen and said, inexorably, "Check."
Carlyle took the offending queen with his eager
king. Kit moved a rook in his own king's row

just three squares sideways. It was an attack from afar and Carlyle had never seen it.

"Shah matte," said Kit.

"I beg pardon?" gulped Carlyle.

It was eight-forty-five. Kit got up. "Shah matte, my friend. "The king is dead."

"You mean he's checkmated?" said Carlyle, trying wildly as losers will to move his king somewhere, anywhere. And everywhere his poor king had to go was adequately covered by some far off, unsuspected and detached-looking piece of Kit's.

"You owe me a hundred," said Kit.

Carlyle sighed and dug for his wallet. As he paid he said, "What's that word you used? Shah matte?"

"It's Persian, a very ancient tongue, from which the word checkmate was originally derived. Shah is for king and matte means dead. The king is dead. Found an old, old book on the game once. Interesting."

"Well, he's certainly very dead at that," said Carlyle ruefully. "But I'll put the hundred on the Arbiter's expense account. It isn't that which worries me. The trouble with chess is that it so drastically reflects the mentality of the player. There's no luck in it whatever and a loss is a direct insult to one's wits. Confound it, Tourney, you make me feel like one of these pawns. You had that all lined up for twenty moves and never sprung it and babe-like I'm gulled to sitting across from you with vast plans of conquest against you. Confound it, I'm going to sit here and get stinko drunk and put it on your bill."

Kit, resplendent in his fresh uniform, straightened himself up and settled the helmet in place. "Don't drink the town dry. I may be back in time to toast you under the table."

"Cheerio," said Carlyle and reached for the phone. He heard the door click behind Kit and then an elevator whine. "Wine!" he told room service. "Champagne, by gad. Three magnums and this is Tourney talking."

He hung up and the phone rang.

"Sir," said the desk, "Colonel Mollyhay of the Greater Triad Emperor's Scientific Own requests audience."

Carlyle frowned and then, alertly looking at the door which Kit had just left, said, "Send the gentleman up. By all means. Send him up." He hung up and reached into his suitcase from which he took a flat gun, shoulder straps dangling from its case. "Hmmm. So he didn't know that space-tramp, eh? Come in. Come in."

Kit noticed nothing unusual in the lobby, but he wasn't taking time to look. He shoved his gold helmet into a cab and said, "Spaceman's Rest and be quick."

He sank back and watched the town's lights sweep swiftly by. Something like an alarm bell was ringing dismally inside his skull and he found his hands were sweating with nervousness. A splendid traffic cop halted their lane for a moment and Kit instinctively ducked.

"Here now," he told himself. "Hold on hard and none of the jumps. You've been in tighter spots before and weaseled out with your neck. Be cool, me bucko, be cool!"

It wasn't very cool in the Spaceman's Rest.

The place was in layers of blue smoke and evil with the ozone fumes of a gun lately fired. The unlucky one was being brought out on an ambulance stretcher as Kit walked in. Groups in booths were beginning to cheer up after the fight. Lazy and heavy-lidded women tinkled through the crowd urging the sale of drinks or picking up a bit of custom on the side. Humanoids, demi-humans and decayed humans were here, all reeking with *dak* and Ole Space Ranger. In an atmosphere no one could breathe, full of drinks no man could digest, telling each other things no mortal should hear, the spacemen were having their version of a very fine time. A sleepy orchestra composed wholly of outlandish fish-scale people sawed outraged notes through the babble and clang.

The uniform caused no comment. Anyone or anything might come here and Kit pursued his search unmolested. He heard an angry argument and found his man.

Spica Mike and his captain, a bearded one named Malloy, were daring the bouncer to try to put them out. And the bouncer was being very reluctant to carry out his threats. This one, a huge Tsarian, was glad to find Kit standing there. It provided a diversion. He left.

Spica Mike said, "If it ain't Kit! Captain Malloy, this here is Kit, the finest fightin' redhead this side of hell's yawning doors. Git on his side in a fight. Ever' time. Always on his side and don't make no mistake. . . ."

"You're drunk," grinned Kit. "And here I had work for sober men."

"Drunk!" said Spica Mike, reeling upright

like a run-down top. "Drunk? Who says we're drunk! Am I drunk, captain?"

"You're drunk," said Captain Malloy, grinning into his whiskers. "Sit down, Kit and be likewise."

"I said work for sober men," said Kit.

"Well, hell, sit down anyway. You can't talk with a dry throat," said Malloy.

"Kit," said Spica Mike, "let's all get drunk."

"Drunkenness," said Kit, "is a psychological state. Liquor is evil for the human system. Alcohol is a depressant, not a stimulant. Make mine *dak*."

"See," said Spica Mike to his captain. "I told you he was a regular. Seen him blow down six Tsarians one night. One, two, three, four, five, six. I never got a chance to strike a blow, so help me. Quick as. . . ."

"You mentioned business," said Malloy. "Murder, kidnapping or arson? We've an idle ship with a low pay cargo and we're cleared for all ports."

"My luck is holding, then," said Kit. "I've just ten thousand dollars that says we clear by midnight with my cargo."

"For ten thousand dollars I'd clear four hours ago," said Malloy. "Spica Mike reads minds. We should have been gone at six but he came back and told me about you and a uniform you didn't own and I smelled business. Here we are."

"Standby with your tubes warming, then," said Kit. "Cargo hatch open. Here's a thousand on account and four when I board and five when I land plus two more for good behavior

58

from my boss when we get there."

"We won't hang, will we?"

"If you hang, I'll raise it to fifteen thousand straight," said Kit, grinning. He threw off the *dak*, shuddered from its stimulant and rose. "Stand by, gentlemen."

He paid their bill and dropped them at the port while he went back to the labs. And there he found a reception committee.

"That's him!" said Colonel Mollyhay.

"All right, General," said an intelligence man. "Come along."

Kit looked at Carlyle standing there in the shadows of the guard gate. He looked at young Mollyhay, angry as a hornet and as red as his uniform with containing it.

Kit looked at Mollyhay. "Salute, you cub!"

"None of that!" said the intelligence man, motioning to the guards.

"Salute!" roared Kit.

Mollyhay's face certainly paled a trifle.

"Aha," said Kit. "The imposter doesn't know the proper salute!"

"I do so!" cried the beleagured Mollyhay and saluted.

"Hmmm. Too studiedly accurate," said Kit. "Where are your credentials?"

Mollyhay fumed but the intelligence man was staring at him and he angrily brought them out. "A confounded farce."

Kit glared at the papers. "Aha! Signed by Adjutant Major Deuchard! Dated this year. Gentlemen, I am glad you apprehended this fellow. Deuchard was an adjutant rightly enough but he's been dead four years to my knowledge and we've no ghosts in the Emperor's Scientific Own. At least none doing adjutant's work. Has this man been in to see the machine?"

"Why, yes," said the intelligence man, getting nervous.

"Then come along," said Kit, "and don't let him escape. We'll see if sabotage has been attempted. Come along, my good fellow and the next time you try to discredit one of our service, study up on your lines and salutes. It may save your life."

Mollyhay was near exploding with rage but it looked like confusion. Kit was already striding off into the yard toward the sacred inner sanctum. Uncertainly the intelligence man tagged along.

"General," said the intelligence man, "I'm sorry to insist but we'll have to ionbeam the Greater Triad with your identification and this officer's. I apologize deeply if there. . . ."

"Certainly, certainly," said Kit. "Send one of your errand boys with orders to do so My credentials are on file at the palace. But meantime, my man, if this imposter has been near the machine, it may blow up any instant with your lone technician in the bargain."

That put haste in them. Even in Carlyle. For Carlyle was getting unsure again. After all, you didn't find a scientific genius amongst the spy riff-raff of the space bagnios.

The pale young man had heard all about it and he looked extremely worried. He did not like the idea of being sold outright to another prison keeper like his own emperor and Kit had given him some hope. Ah, to see a pretty girl again! But not under the Arbiter he wouldn't.

The machine was in the bright moonlight of Ringo's dumb-bell moons. The pale young man had tinkered around with detectors until he had a fine vein.

"Has this fellow been in this machine?" said Kit, wink, wink.

"Why he hasn't . . ." wink, wink received, "he hasn't missed, general." And suddenly the pale young man shook at his temerity. He had not really supposed anything was wrong but these winks. . . . Why was he playing the game with maybe a spy?

"Get in there and search!" cried Kit with all anxiety. And he plunged in after the pale young man.

Carlyle alone guessed it. And he acted too late.

There was a roar, a flash and the machine shuddered. The intelligence man yelled and a guard drew a gun. But there was just a hole where the machine had stood.

The intelligence man leaned over the pit, buffeted by the wind roaring up from it. "Come up out of that!" he yelled idiotically. "Come on back here!"

Carlyle was forced to grin. "Should have known," he mused. "No high brass would be that clever to beat me at chess."

"After him!" cried the intelligence and Mollyhay together.

"Don't bother," said Carlyle with a wicked smile. "I've taken care to procure all his actual

61

data down to fingerprints. They'll be on the way to the Arbiter by dawn and every system in the galaxy will be plastered with his picture Red hair, you know."

"What's red hair got to do with it?" howle intelligence.

"Conspicuous. Awful error to send a man an intelligence mission with red hair. The was a slip at the spaceport. After that I too the data down. Be calm, gentlemen."

They went frenzied at the sound of a spa ship roaring out of the port.

"Be calm," said Carlyle with a wicked yaw "Nobody can escape the Arbiter. Nobody. I see to it personally that you both get word that young man's execution, so I will. Be cal gentlemen."

He looked at the bright stars where plum of flame were just now fading.

"Your first name's Kit," said Carlyle. "T Arbiter knows how to canvas the unive sities. Yes, indeed, my friend. We'll meet a then. . . ."

Chapter Seven

WHEN CHRISTOPHER RANDOLPH KELLAN HAD
finished giving his verbal report to Peter Vanpoll, that worthy nodded twice, perkily, looked
somewhat harassed and went to the casement
of the tower from which he had a remarkable
view of the Gulf of Batabano and the remarkable distant mountains of Cuba.

"Carlyle, eh?" said Vanpoll at last. "Kellan,
you were certainly breathing on the Arbiter's
hand. When the work's the dirtiest, when the
deal smells of bribery and graft, when trembling governments are about to leave their
foundations and fall in upon their people, you'll
find Carlyle. He is an assistant councilman.
This project then was something more important than I'd realized. Well, to work. You'll
find we've something of a laboratory down below. This old Spanish fort once was honey-
combed with dungeons below the tide mark;

you'll find they're all laboratory now. I have a project for you to. . . ."

"Whoa!" said Kit, giving the golden helmet a push with his fist. "I've been off on a mighty fatiguing journey. I've had the extra fat fried out of me from nerves and exhaustion. I served as a tubeman first class all the way down here, watch and watch, we were so short of hands. And if you've tried to live on a can like that we've just sent away, you'll understand. . . ."

"I understand only that we're pushed for time," said Vanpoll coolly. "We need a certain type of weapon. . . ."

"Weapon?" And Kit sank back, tunic collar flying loose. "My dear Mr. Vanpoll, that is one thing you won't get from me. Doubtless you have very clever engineers, much cleverer than myself. But as to weapons—no!"

"Why not?"

"I am a half-fledged engineer, well read it is true, but only an engineer. My mission as a scientist is to benefit mankind. I can see no benefit arising from the tailoring of some hot blast to murder and cripple my fellow men. No, no and tut, tut, Mr. Vanpoll. No weapons."

Vanpoll looked hard at him and hostility seemed to crackle about them and between them.

"Mr. Kellan, as an agent of the P.R.S. you will follow orders."

"Mr. Vanpoll, as a mainspring of the P.R.S. you ought to know better than to ask an engineer for a weapon. I'll perform the errands you elect and steal this Arbiter blind or even attempt against him personally, but I'll make no weapon of which I myself do not have the use."

Vanpoll snorted. "My dear sir," he said in a way which meant Kit was anything but his dear sir, "the weapon upon which you were to work is directly connected to your next job. There's a shipment of the Arbiter's we must have. . . ."

"Must we talk of my next job?"

The coolness about him thickening up to ice, Vanpoll said, "We must. For you have to understand, Kellan, once and for all, that I'll not allow you to stew about here in idleness. There's little enough time. You have certain tasks and then you will attempt the Arbiter himself. Thus it. . . ."

"Aha," said Kit. "Carla."

"I fear I do not understand you."

"I fear I do not believe you," said Kit.

"Listen, my redheaded friend, personalities. . . ."

"Are such that you don't intend to let me spoon around with Carla. I've had a lot of time to think, Mr. Vanpoll, and I've thought some remarkable thoughts. You had me badly off balance when first I joined you. Threatening to dump me with a murdered S.B.I. man and so forth. And you can send me out as target for the day for the Arbiter's crew. But you can't tell me not to see Carla."

"It would be unfair," said Vanpoll. "See here, my friend, you are strictly blaster bait. You're young and good-looking. Carla is a fine girl. Do you want to snare her heart, cause her to pattern her whole life for you and then get killed? You wouldn't do that to a woman."

"Nope. I've no intention of getting killed. As for the rest of it I think it is a very wonderful idea. Where is she?"

"I order you to go to the labs and put this new technician to work on a weapon."

"Order away. I'll say hello to Carla and get out of this monkey suit before I'll think a single thought for you and your lab. My God, man. I've just been across a hundred and ninety light years of space, dodging patrol cruisers and intelligence men, sleeping with both eyes open and you deny me so much as a moment to bathe. Come now, revolution can wait while Kellan washes the body. And I won't make a weapon."

"Not for your own use?"

"That depends on how badly I'll need it."

"Well," shrugged Vanpoll, "my control over you is obviously limited."

"I am a very strong-headed young man. From space skipper to college professor, they've told me so."

"I wash my hands of this!" cried the beleaguered Vanpoll.

"You need me," said Kit, "and you'll humor me."

"Go find Carla then. Go find her! But so help me, Kellan, if you're not in that lab by noon, you'll be sorry!"

"He lost dramatically," said Kit and got up to go.

"Devil take you," said Vanpoll. "But when you learn your next orders, and realize that you've only until tomorrow to make all preparations to leave, you'll wish you hadn't bucked me. Get out."

Kit got.

Chapter Eight

HE DID NOT FIND CARLA, SHE FOUND HIM. He was just finishing the knot of sash as the final touch when he had a premonition and turned. His heart skipped a beat.

She was wearing her wine tunic and her hair was soft as a summer night. The way she held ˉ head, the delicate gesture of her hand, the way she walked . . . the things she made a man think of. . . .

"Kit! You came through it!"

He wasn't aware of words. The voice, though was most soothing. Listening for more he felt the touch of her hands on his arms and he stopped listening. She looked at him, drinking him in.

"Was it dreadful?" she asked.

There was a long pause and then he said, "Beg pardon?"

"You goose! Tell me or I'll shake you!"

"That's a good idea," said Kit, the facility of his mind turning this into "I'll kiss you." And he did so. And they stood in a gold and perfumed haze which went around and around and around and lasted so long that Henry had to cough five times and slam the door twice to break through the dream.

"Mister Kellan, I do beg your pardon and I wouldn't disturb you under any ordinary circumstance, but Mr. Vanpoll just this minute reached the top of the landing and personally, what with Mr. Vanpoll's. . . ." He gaped, teeth shining in a slack mouth. And then he gently shut the door. He said to Vanpoll, "He just don't seem to be there, sir."

Vanpoll looked baffled but Henry was awfully big.

"See here, Henry. It isn't I you thwart. But somebody won't be pleased. . . ."

"Love," said Henry, "is something which doesn't ask anybody's permission."

"But good Lord, Henry. You don't understand that that young man. . . ."

"I understand that a young man is just a young man so long," said Henry. "Let's go look for them in the laboratory, Mr. Vanpoll." And he walked forward with such remorseless bulk that Vanpoll went down the stairs, muttering awful things about mutiny and sedition and ingratitude.

They found, when they had turned the coral-arched passage that their new addition was already on the job. Very caressingly the pale young man was setting up his brainchild and eying a fissure of granite which was part of the ancient dungeon in which the lab was situated.

"What's your name?" said Vanpoll nastily.

The pale young man was much blown back. "Young, sir. Technician Young, late of the Engineers of the Emperor of Ringo."

"What's that you're doing?"

"Why, sir, this is the machine the general and I built and stole. I guess it was stealing."

"The general is not a general," said Vanpoll. "He is one of our agents. Are you prepared to join the People's Revolutionary Society and assist us in the overthrow of a despot?"

"I don't understand, sir. I'm sorry."

"The Arbiter with his Intergalactic Bank and his Arbitration Council. . . ."

"No, no," said the young man. "I don't understand about joining anything or anybody. I don't even want to be enlisted. I'm tired of being told 'Do this,' or 'Do that,' and then being caged up because I did it and can't be trusted."

"Young," said Vanpoll, "we can be very severe. I must insist that you join us."

"Sir," said the young man doggedly, "I can't because already I've got myself committed."

"How is this?" cried Peter Vanpoll.

"I'm working for the general."

"He's no general!"

Young smiled. "I don't care about that. He's a general where I'm concerned and if he happens to be working for you, that's his business. But I happen to be working for him. No, he didn't ask me and we haven't even mentioned pay. But mister, I'm working for the general

70

even if he pays me nothing." And with a determination quite foreign to him he turned his back on Peter Vanpoll and went back to tinkering with the machine.

Henry grinned as Vanpoll retreated to the steps and sat down.

"What the deuce are you grinning about?" cried Vanpoll.

"Well sir, it just seems to me that Mr. Kit. . . ."

"You be quiet!"

The huge Negro became quiet. But there was no authority on earth or in space that could keep him from grinning.

After a long time, Christopher Randolph Kellan, walking with great bouyancy—for he tread on altocumulus and not on ground at all —came down to the lab, arm in arm with Carla.

"Yes, sir!" said Kit with a salute. "Here I am, twelve sharp."

"It's one-thirty," said Vanpoll.

"That's what he said," said Carla. "One-thirty sharp."

"You, too," said Vanpoll, and he looked heavenward for forgiveness on the assembled. But homehow he pulled himself together, shot his cuffs, straightened his pearl stick-pin, smoothed his hair and brought order to the proceedings. "Mr. Kellan, you've very little time and the job is very dangerous. You are required to take charge of a cargo that the Arbiter is shipping to Marfak's Kile. It will have to be done on the wing. . . ."

Kit heard him out, growing sober as he listened. Then he said, "What is on this ship that's so important, Mr. Vanpoll?"

"Neutroneum catalyst. About seventy-five million dollars of it. Its purpose is to strengthen Marfak's position as a buffer state for the Arbiter's particular purposes and to incidentally take away that seventy-five million dollars from the already impoverished people of the Marfak System. The catalyst is, as you may know, a necessity for the manufacture of munitions. We need it and the purpose is not so much to deny it to the Marfak System as it is to procure it for our future operating capital. To be blunt, we need finance. The catalyst will sell anywhere, you know, in small or large amounts. Your purpose is to devise a means to stop a space-ship in mid-flight without destroying her cargo."

"You want the catalyst intact?" said Kit. "Would you be as interested in denying it to Marfak?"

"That's immaterial. Don't get ideas of destroying ship and cargo."

"Ah," said Kit. "Well, folks, my lengthy vacation is over." And he reached for a lead apron and smiled at Young.

They withdrew but Carla came back soon, having bribed the Chinese to permit her to carry the lunch down. She found a very mysterious conference which gave her no heed, Kit and Young muttering formulas like two witch doctors, holding electrodes instead of thigh bones. She felt neglected and went away only to return at six with supper which, to her

72

surprise turned out to be very welcome in that they had not seen or eaten the lunch. But just as Kit was beginning to smile at her he had another idea, dropped his plate and went into another conference with Young. Disgusted she withdrew.

Until one o'clock she lingered at the head of the stairs, playing fantan with the Chinese guard and losing much to his amusement, for she held key sevens, and then seeing no sign of Kit, gave it up and went to bed.

At six the next morning her tuned ear heard the dungeon doors open and wrapping herself in negligee, hurried to the top of the steps. She did not go down for there was Vanpoll in his bathrobe and Kit smeared with dust and soot in his apron and his last thought was for her, it seemed.

"Well, we got it, Mr. Vanpoll."

"Fine, fine! What system are you going to use? Tractor beams . . . ?"

"No, no, no," said Kit. "We got IT!"

Young and the hastily summoned Henry were staggering up the steps under heavy loads. They dumped piles of sacks and went back for more.

"What's this?" cried Vanpoll.

"Why, that's seventy-five million dollars worth of neutroneum catalyst."

"But . . . how?"

"Why we took the lead shielding off the vibratron and used the lead. . . ."

"No, no! I mean now. . . ."

"Now," said Kit in triumph, "I can stick around and rest up. I figured it was a long

73

way up to Marfak and if all you wanted was the catalyst, why Young and I worked out the basic pattern of. . . ."

"No you don't!" cried Vanpoll, looking straight up at Carla who was leaning over the rail with the beginnings of a radiant smile on her face. "No you don't, sir! I've just the past hour . . . er . . . received word that one of our . . . agents was killed and that the people's revolt on Darengo was decimating the populace. You get up there this instant and stop that war."

"Stop . . . ?"

"Yes. Get up to Darengo and stop the war. You leave . . . it's just six-ten now. You leave at eight. You can sleep while Henry flies. He's going all the way with you."

Chapter Nine

At eight the small, wicked Mark 89 Raider slid out of the coral cavern through huge watertight doors and into the pale emerald gleam of the undersea world. Propelled by her landing tractors only, the sleek ship eased up to thirty fathoms and sped forward a hundred and five miles an hour, heading for the Misteriosa Bank in the western Caribbean from which she could launch safely and unseen into the fastnesses of space.

Kit watched the marine gardens flee below and though the slow-motion riot of growth and fish offered many a fascinating sight, Kit sulked.

"That's all right, Mister Kit," said Henry, settling back in the pilot's seat now that he had settled on course. "She'll wait. She'll wait."

"But will I last?" muttered Kit. "There doesn't seem to be any end of the ways Vanpoll can get me out of there and sooner or later this sort of business is likely to prove dangerous."

"Don't worry, Mister Kit. Pluck will see you through and the more you fret the lesser gets your chances. Chino and me are with you this trip and we'll take good care of you." He eyed his compass, in a very unhandy spot so little was it used on a space ship, and decided to put Kit to work. "You know, Mister Kit, I ain't never had any trouble driving or flying anything you engineers put together. But I do get a little bit hazy on three dimensional navigation. If you wants to do us a favor and make sure we arrive at the Darengo System or whichever we're going, I'd most certainly appreciate a course for departure when we leave the sea."

Kit rose and went into the small chartroom where tropical sunlight, filtered through thirty fathoms of crystal sea water, painted the overhead nav turret dark green and gave the space charts a strange cast. It made Kit feel eerie to be quartermastering under the sea instead of in the normal of star-studded inky space.

The United Planets Spacographic Office Star Pilot, Systems C to E, had a sketchy article on the Darengo System. Space and weight being what they were on a Mark 89 Raider, no further data was available. But Kit gathered that the system was off track and was considerably retarded from former greatness, listing yards with cradles for unlimited tonnage and then changing, in 3974 supplement to "reported to be of unknown repair, larger cradles abandoned." In fact, practically everything in the nine planet system was corrected in reduction.

Kit spread his orders to the pale-green, flickering light and read the hasty pen scratches with which Vanpoll had dismissed him.

"Will proceed to Saint Martin, capital city of Saint Martin Planet, Darengo System where as an ambassador of the Kingdom of Kauburn will protest destruction of property of Kauburn citizens and while this cover lasts effect a cessation of hostilities and a restoration of the Republic under one Montpelier, decently elected but forcefully deposed president. Arbiter seeks military rule under one General Francisco Gomez y Caveda de Batille. Assassination of said Francisco etc. not desirable. Contact Loring, Standard Uranium Co. of Terra for funds and assistance. Return and report in person at earliest date. P.V."

Dutifully, Kit looked up Saint Martin and found, "Carbon planet, oxygen 4/5 atmo.; 9.8871; temperate zone at poles; rot. 26.9 hrs. 31 mi. 2 secs.; yr. 961 days 23 hrs.; axis tilt 1° 5 secs.; 349,000,000 mi. circ. orb.;" and like material which gave him a fairly good idea of the climate and conditions without any further description, space being precious in star pilot. "Saint Mart, Capital City, located exactly at positive pole, major vessel repairs, some types of fuels, ice and fresh water, compressed atmosphere available, limited stores, marine hospital, naval base of Darengo System. Maintains shops for repair of war vessels (cor. now in dismantled condition). Distinguishable by many ancient bldgs. in radiant design and lies between two oceans, the Peters Sea and the Outland Sea. Landing beams of Alpha des. (now in disuse). Customs and immigration punctilious (now abandoned). Display Darengo System National Lights on level with own nationality (now not enforced). Warning: St. M. Equatorial belt is swamp from 50° N. Lat. to 50° S. Lat., inhabited by unknown but dangerous fauna, of intolerable heat and without rescue stations. Avoid."

"Nice place," said Kit glumly. He looked up the star, Darengo, and found it to be 3 x Sun, orange, .4573 surf. heat units and in the 23° hub sector, Zone 297. "Traveling at 12½ m.p.sec. on course 24° hub sector, at Zone pos. 297.6312 in Oct. 3972. Beware 326 comets and heavy meteor swarms Darengo area."

Kit applied the space-hemisphere, looked up his tables, computed the position of Earth, the position of Sun and then in the spherical tables found the course to the Galactic Hub, an ideal center. He then computed the present moment's position of Darengo, corrected for length of flight and its course and distance from Hub. The secondary tables gave him the translation of Point A to Point C without reference to Point B, the Hub, and then, recorrecting for the actual time run at 933 lt. yrs., had his answer. "Hub 93°, Dip 71° 17' 14.4445."

"Be there in 8.091 days," said Kit. "I left a retabulation of runs for any day in the next five months running in the computer so that you will have your tape if anything happens to me."

Henry nodded appreciatively, just as though

he had not graduated from the Spacographer's School at Lawrence, Kansas, during his service as a Master Gunner in the United Planets' Space Force.

"What do they have?" said Henry.

"Oh, fresh water, ice, common fuel. . . ."

"No, no. Mister Kit, I don't want to take a perfectly dry, unemotional sort of liberty up there."

"Well, it didn't mention wine, women and song," said Kit. "And as near as I can make out the whole place is falling down around their ears."

"Hmmm," said Henry. "War. That does it, war. Nobody never won a war, Mister Kit. You'd think man'd learn that."

"Sorry you've got such a dull time ahead," said Kit, close to sarcasm.

"Oh, no sir, Mister Kit. War is a sort of catalyst. It brings out the beast in women. Hold on tight, sir. Here we go."

The take-off gongs rang through the ship. Her own gravity plates wrenched against Earth's pull on the crew. Then, nose sweeping upward in a wash of silver foam, she leaped from the sea and the roaring drives sent great piles of steam and spray to hang whitely above the Caribbean's blue. At seven *g's* she spurned Earth and air and her ports went black when the stars came out. Savagely accelerating, she whipped to her course, quivering in every plate like a sensitive animal under spur and left the Solar System behind her.

When her bow gravity pulls had taken the curse off her forward surgings, Kit walked aft, gazed after by the five man crew who were leaving their take-off stations to settle themselves into watches for the long grind. The Chinese, Sailor Ah Wing as he was called, had coffee and cigarettes waiting in the wardroom. Kit sat down at the green covered board, the familiar whine of fuel feeds trembling in the overhead ducts, the low whisper of the airmakers monotonous in his ears. The Chinese put out some cheddar cheese and crackers.

"Don't be discouraged, Mr. Kellan," he said. "It's a long voyage which has no ending."

"I'm up to my ears in philosophers," said Kit grumpily. "If Vann∙'l keeps me riding around in the stars lik∙ ∙. I'll be able to breathe in a vacuum and wal∙ on comets' tails."

"We will get this over rapidly," said Sailor Ah Wing. "Merely indicate who is to be mourned at the funeral." He tapped his shoulder gun and grinned, eyes very merry.

"Revolution hardens one," said Kit. "But just what we're really doing and why is a thing which puzzles me exceedingly. Just what is the Arbiter's object, Sailor?"

The Chinese masked his eyes and his grin became false. "These are problems for greater minds, Mr. Kellan. Me, I just shoot." He made a motion at his gun and twitched his finger twice, "Bing, Bing! You drink your coffee."

Kit thought about it for a little while. He didn't know why he was doing what he did. If those people didn't have him so solidly. . . . And then he gave it up and watched the stars creep slowly by. It was so much easier to think of Carla.

80

But he couldn't concentrate. There was a tink-tink-tink outside the hull where somebody in a space suit was already changing the ship's designation to the Kingdom of Kauburn's five red lights and eight blue, inner and outer circle. Young looked in, very pale, dreadfully space-sick. Young saw the cheddar cheese and crackers and moved hastily out again.

Kit gloomed. They certainly had him in tight. He looked at the pile of passports, papers and bulletins which would make him an ambassador from Kauburn. With sudden energy he picked them up and began his studies. The sooner done, the sooner he'd see Carla.

Chapter Ten

WHATEVER KIT HAD EXPECTED TO FIND, HE was disappointed. When they'd worn out their patience for an entire day waiting for a tug to come out and pull them down to the postage stamp spaceport they could televise through the low-hanging clouds, they decided that this was one planet which didn't care how many tons of unwieldy ship came plummeting down at its capital city and went on in, be damned to the regulations.

They stood on their tails and sat down, plowing up frightful quantities of already blast-blackened ground, finding themselves in a pleasantly warm atmosphere with a very cool reception.

Saint Martin's source of light and heat, Darengo, stood about twenty degrees high, it being about noon. It sank down to eighteen and rose to twenty-two degrees but it never sank under the horizon. The shadows were long on Saint Martin, always long, and they traveled three hundred and sixty degrees around you without ever vanishing. About three degrees above the horizon crept three moons which often rose as high as thirty degrees and as often vanished palely from sight or disappeared in their phases. It was a crazy world of crouching trees and spiring buildings all running out in radiant, militant lines from the spaceport. Once it may have been glorious but decay was here like a vulture on its prey. The naval dock was a shell of rubble. The custom house was a temporary shack squatting on the ruins of the old operations building. A guard sat in darengo, idly watching two one-pound flies tear up the papers of his finished lunch.

Kit climbed down the ladder, stumbling on the hem of his ambassador's gown, portfolio gripped in hand and a grey Kauburn hat in the other. The hat was much too small for him and he would not wear it.

"Hello," he said to the guard.

That one looked up, raised his brows a little and seemed on the verge of speaking. But he changed his mind and fell to watching the flies.

"Where is everybody?" said Kit.

"I reckon you won't have any luck, stranger, if you expect a welcoming committee. We're too busy." He fell to watching flies again.

"Where is the president?"

"If you mean General Batille, why I guess he's in the government house. Or maybe he ain't. The troops is gone, you know."

"Ah. So?"

"They're down chasin' Recalcitrants around the swamps."

"Where're the people?"

The guard looked at Kit in pity. "The people? Why, crawlin' bedbugs, stranger, them's the Recalcitrants."

"Do I enter my landing here?"

"No. Heck, we dispensed with that nonsense long time ago. All I'm supposed to do is to see that nobody steals anything off the field. And don't try it neither," he added with sudden emphasis. But the mood faded and he became interested in the flies once more and no number of questions would extract further reply from him.

Kit hoofed it toward a tall building, about a half a kilometer from the port. In the distance it appeared to be of solid silver but on closer approach, it was obvious that the plating was chipped and peeled until more of it was off than on.

A soldier with a red handkerchief around his arm as his sole badge was playing with a small dog in front of the doors.

"Where can I find General Batille?" said Kit.

The soldier jerked a thumb at the doors and went on playing with the dog.

The elevator was out of order and Kit was blowing heavily by the time he reached the sixteenth floor. His footfalls rang hollowly through the structure and no one was visible to give him directions. Thus, quite unintentionally as he poked through the dusty, disused offices, he walked unannounced into the presence of General Batille.

The general was a small man, heavily loaded with insignia and a mop of stand-up black hair. He was very stiff as he stood at the window employing a field glass on some distant object and he leaped half out of his wits when he caught sight of Kit in the door.

Kit looked at the thick rug, the heavy desk and the straight slant-eyed general. "Excuse me, I was looking for General Batille."

There was something hunted about the man. He tip-toed to the door and closed it. "Who are you?"

Kit was about to say he was an ambassador when a sixth sense made him hold his peace.

"How did you get through the cordon?" demanded Batille.

"I wasn't aware there was one," said Kit. "When the ship landed. . . ."

"Ah! The ship! You've brought the money, then."

"Well . . ." began Kit.

"I've produced it. I've carried out my part of the bargain. The place is a wrecked ruin and the last of the people are so deep in the swamp they'll never win free. I've kept my bargain. Now where is the money?"

"I must have evidence," said Kit.

"Of course, of course. But you came from the port and you saw the town. There's not a human being in it except my soldiers. Not even a cat. I've wiped it clean with great thoroughness. Down in the southern hemisphere there's not a hamlet inhabited. Here there's no one alive outside of the great swamps. Now how much did you bring?"

"Quite enough," said Kit, his mind working very fast. "But I am curious as to why the port isn't guarded. People could land."

"Not from this system. We've spread rumors of disease and no one could penetrate the force screen until I turned it off for you this morning. As soon as you called for a tug I knew who you were and had it turned off. But here, make your inspection of my records and reports. The place has no inhabitants. The mines are entirely free. I've executed the engineers and I hold Loring of Standard Uranium a hostage. It has taken me three long years to wreck Saint Martin. Now I want my pay."

"You'll get everything you deserve," said Kit. "Believe me, General Batille, you will." From the window he could look down into the court and there was a seared wall there with black spots at its base. "But are your officers to be trusted?"

"The scum of space. Pirates, drunkards, yellow ticket men all. There's not a decent human being in the entire army. I should know. I recruited it myself. And now, if we make a fast inspection I . . . well, I would like to be going."

"I'll take your word," said Kit. "You wouldn't lie about a thing like that. Come out to my ship and we'll give you everything in the bargain."

Batille put on a small helmet, mashing down his bristling hair. He set his buck teeth in an anticipatory grin and he bowed Kit out. Arm in arm they went down the wide silver stairs, past broken vases in the niches and cracked paintings on the walls.

The soldier at the door stood up, looking frightened and the dog cowered back.

"Not a bad town," said Kit.

"You are welcome to it," said Batille. "Have you any idea of how it is trying to live under the strain I've been under? Treachery, foul treachery at every hand. Until I invented the force screen cordon, I could scarcely sleep nights. But now we're safe in here. Not even a rat could get into the city. But let's walk faster, my friend. I'll not be sorry to get my pay."

They came to the port where the Mark 89 Raider stood and Batille grinned in admiration. "Kauburn flag. That's clever, very clever. I wouldn't have suspected it myself. Ha, Ha!" And he leaped nimbly up the ladder to the open port. "Ah, I can taste the fine wines now. I can almost feel the hands of pretty women. A few months of fast living and I'll be ready for you again." He was blinking his eyes, accustoming them to the dimness of the interior, having stared Darengo in the eye when he boarded.

The gun in his ribs was a sudden stab. His mouth was bruised by Kit's strong left hand while the belt radio transmitter was jerked off and smashed.

Kit threw the man away from him into the arms of the astonished Sailor Ah Wing.

"What's this?" screamed Batille in terror.

"This is General Batille, Sailor. Put him in

triple irons. I'll want to find out what rotten dog hired him to tear a planet to bits in the name of revolution. Don't be gentle!"

Sailor Ah Wing wasn't. He threw Batille into a spare storeroom which would also serve as a brig and began to tie him up very tightly with extremely puzzling knots.

"How is this?" wailed Batille. "Oh, you blackguard!" And "Give me back my radio and you'll sing another tune. I'll have ten thousand men upon you in an hour! They know I'm gone and where I've gone for I opened the dial when I said where. They'll be here, I tell you!"

"Who hired you?" said Kit.

"I'll have your heart. I'll cut it. . . ."

"Sailor, isn't there some method by which he might be made to listen to reason?"

There was, Sailor thought, and Kit went into the wardroom to get a drink of water. Henry was in the passage, big-eyed.

"Who you got?"

"Batille."

"Batille the chief man here? Oh my Lord!" His eyes got big at Kit. "Mister Kit, you surely are the fastest man I ever heard tell of any-place. My gonnies!" And he went to find the crew and tell them quick to man everything the Raider boasted that would work like a weapon.

Kit came back and Batille was conscious again and most amazingly willing to talk. There wasn't a mark on him either.

"Who employed you?" said Kit.

"Take this yellow devil off me!"

"Yellow devil yourself," said Sailor, doing

something with his hand.

Batille woke up shortly. "Universal Uranium Limited of course!"

"Did you ever hear of the Arbiter?" said Kit.

"The . . . the Arbiter?"

"Yes. Speak up now. Go ahead, Sailor."

"No, no. I know the Arbiter. I didn't know he was behind Universal Uranium. How was I to know?" And then a new thought struck him. "I'm ruined! If I've failed the Arbiter. . . . But I didn't know I was working for him. I swear I didn't. Tell me I wasn't. Please tell me. If it was the Arbiter he'll search all space for me. Nobody can escape the Council. Nobody ever has! Tell me it wasn't the Arbiter." And he went off into shuddering sobs, much more injured now than he had been by Sailor Ah Wing.

"Lock him in," said Kit, tearing off the black robe and getting his hip gun in position. He took down a helmet and picked up a box of tools. "Young! You, Henry. Get me Young quick. This man was no fool. His officers may be in town and they'll know. . . ."

"Where you going?" cried Henry.

"Back to the palace where we can straighten this thing out. Come on, Young."

"No, no, Kit!" cried Henry. "Strong arm ain't your department. Don't you dare walk in and. . . ."

"You'll stay here," said Kit crisply. "If I want you, Young's radio will serve and then come running with your guns ready. But until then, this is my game."

"Oh, woe! Stop him, Sailor. He don't know. . . ."

Kit was already on the ground, Young panting to keep up with him.

"Murder thousands . . . hunt them into swamps . . . burn hamlets . . ." Kit was muttering. "What a rotten, filthy deal! Oh, wait until I get my hands on that Arbiter! Just wait! Come on here, Young. Good Lord, can't you move any faster than that?"

Chapter Eleven

THE DOOR GUARD WAS MISSING WHEN KIT and Young pounded into the palace. Breathlessly Young struggled up the wide silver staircase, past the cracked vases and scorched murals, barely keeping the flying heels of his "general" in view. He, Young, was gasping and spent when they reached the sixteenth floor.

A quick backstep by Kit displayed that the office was now occupied again. A tall, barrel-bodied officer of singularly filthy appearance was going through papers while he waited for his chief.

Kit signaled Young to keep back and then, gun drawn, stepped through the door. The officer started up in surprise, snatching at his own gun. There was a flash of flame and Young worriedly looked in.

The officer was falling to his knees, then to

his hands, a blank look of amazement spreading across his face. Abruptly he caved in and moved no more.

"Check those communicators," said Kit. "I want to know where they lead. . . . Hello! What's this?" And he stared at the uppermost message on the dispatch spindle.

It was a common intra-system dispatch relayed from the key signal station of the Darengo group. It had been decoded and a fair copy was pinned to it.

From: Universal Uranium
To: General Batille.
Via: Faubourg-Darengo Relay.
OUR REPRESENTATIVE COMING YOUR RELIEF. WELL DONE.

Kit pocketed the message and began to search for more. This explained much to him— the unguarded back door of the city, the eagerness of Batille to talk with him about money—

"Think I've got it," said Young. "Who do you want?"

"The force cordon. Take this loop and locate the directional response." He brought a coil of taline wire from his case, gave it to Young and then buzzed the force cordon.

Young read his belt impulse meter and twisted the hand-held coil. It was crude but in a moment he could say, "Seems like it's straight down this street here about two kilometers."

"Let's go," said Kit, stepping over the dead officer and checking his gun loads for spares to fit his own.

"Won't somebody . . . ?" said Young, pointing to the dead man.

Kit grabbed a boot and towed the man into a closet. Then they were pounding downstairs again, Kit remorselessly leading Young by half a hurried block.

The city was eerie with silence and desertion. Where commerce had thronged and signs blazed there was only desolation, ruined buildings, rifled warehouses and here and there a sprawling dead man neglected even by the well sated flies. Walls leaned crazily into the street, unsettled by bombings. Furniture hung forlornly through missing sections of an apartment house.

Batille had spoken the truth. Not even a cat was moving in Saint Martin.

A guard was sleeping outside the force cordon center. The building was a power relay station, originally, perverted with the rest of its chain to this use. Kit reversed his gun, lifted the edge of the guard's helmet and deepened his sleep considerably.

Inside, amongst a maze of temporary wirings, relays and boosters, lighted up by the snapping, lazy arc of the beamed dynatrodes sat two mechanics. They were obviously ex-pirates, *dak* bloated and slovenly. But there was nothing wrong with their reflexes when they saw Kit.

"What the dog do you want?" said one, starting to rise.

Kit hit him very square and drove a left into the belly of the second in the same consecutive motion. Kit's gun came up and came

93

down four times and the guards were not interested in what he wanted any more.

"Gee," said Young. "You got me spooked. I never seen. . . ."

"I'm mad," said Kit. "I'm mad clean through. You saw this town. You saw what's happened. All for a few dirty dollars. Oh, I'll tell you *he's* not going to hear the last of this."

It was the first time Young had realized that Kit, a redhead, could get red-headed.

"Get on this," said Kit. "What's its wave length? It's a common magnetic magnification stepped up about six million times, I think, counting these coils."

Young measured and told him.

"Can't do it," said Kit. "The other relays around the town wouldn't respond. Can we beam a quarter centimeter wave?"

Young had him then and they worked strenuously and without lost motion. When they had finished the guts of the original installation were strewn about them, stripped down. Kit looked at the dynatrodes. A quarter centimeter radar wave was cracking through them down, beamed as before but oh how deadly. It was a common reduction for this type of installation but it was backed now, not to provide wireless power but to impulse ninety-three million kilovolts. The place began to fry of ozone as the very air broke down.

"Let's get out of here," said Young, shaken.

Kit scooped up a military defense chart of the town which was posted on a table for use when this had been a command post. He drank up details and went off swiftly.

At the first munitions dump they made a "sunfuse," to detonate as soon as Darengo came three degrees around the corner, and then raced away from there to the next dump within the cordon.

They were setting the setting when the first went. A huge, flashing plume of explosives went racking skyward, dulling the darengo light. Masonry pattered down briefly.

The second went and then a third, fourth and fifth in rapid order. The sixth consisted of mines used for ground incinerating and the stacked discs, intended to ignite each one a hundred square yards of dirt and keep it burning for days, promised Kit a fine beacon. They set a five degree fuse and then sprinted for the center of town.

Behind them the very sky fell in. The building itself did not burn, it molecularized and sent every tortured atom of masonry straight about in a column which climbed and climbed .oward a hundred miles, a column very black, ⁺ʷᵖⁱʳ⁓ ⁱⁿto itself as it rose and flashing deep ly inside as though it contained tens of thoʋᶜᵘsands of storms.

Young steadied himself upon the tipping and shaking ground and saw that it hadn't affected Kit. Young followed, worn out with this running but faithful to his last breath.

Back in the palace, from which several windows had been blown, Kit searched under the chips of glass to gather up everything he could find that looked like evidence. He shoved them at Young and to the top of the pile added the Universal Merchants' Code Book.

"There's a ship landing!" said Young.

Kit stared at the big space-craft which was blasting and rising and settling again into the port. "That's hostile. Radio them so on ours."

Kit flung himself down the steps again and did not stop at the street floor. He had seen the gratings from the outside and he hoped he would find what he wanted.

The guard jumped up out of a chair and then slumped against the wall and slid down. Kit holstered his gun, snatched up keys still hot from the blast and unlocked the master unit of the cells.

The middle-aged, haggard gentleman in the second cell was Loring of Standard Uranium, he said.

"Never mind who I am except that I'm from the P.R.S.," said Kit. And although Loring frowned and tried to interrupt, Kit flung a string of information at him, shoved the guard's blaster into his hands, wished him well and got out of there.

The sound of firing was coming from the port and Kit found Young standing agape in the street, watching the battle through openings in the buildings.

"Something's wrong. They're attacking us!" cried Young.

"Run," said Kit. And set the example himself, tearing down the avenue toward the port.

A space ship on the ground, if subjected to the concentrated fire of another at close range, is likely to suffer. The Mark 89 Raider was suffering. Smoke was pouring from its ports and its guns had stopped firing. From its off side came three men, deserting it to its fate. One was seriously wounded and was being carried by another. They were being raked by small arms from the larger vessel.

They would not have made the cover of the wrecked naval depot if Kit had not given them a diversion. He ran into plain sight at the corner of the operations shack, saw the guard there dead from the first major blast concussion and scooped up his long barreled riot gun. Offering himself as a target, Kit snipe-shot the turrets of the big space vessel which quickly turned from undefended game to spray a concentrated fire at this mad newcomer.

Two turrets were blasted in by Kit's fire, the riot gun sending out chains of tomato-red, exploding balls. And then Kit wasn't there and the shack was burning and falling into itself.

From behind a ruined wall, Kit cautiously peered forth, rubbing dirt from his face from his precipitate plunge. The three survivors of the Mark 89 Raider were not in sight. Dust and smoke from the newcomer's shell bursts hid that ship wholly from view for the next several minutes.

Kit dragged his town defense chart into view and studied it through smoke-stung eyes and there Young found him.

"I need ammonia," said Kit.

"Those new shell pits . . ." said Young.

"Good," and he dragged forth what he needed from their tool box.

They worked hurriedly and not, it is to be feared, very thoroughly. For they could hear the doors and ports of the space vessel opening and the mutter of voices in this unnaturally still atmosphere. They bled the riot gun for charges and with mud, dug out with their helmets, they created a miniature furnace. In something under ten minutes, though it seemed a great deal longer to them, Kit had what he wanted, a spray gun of sufficient power charged to the hilt with a powder which, the instant it was diffused in the air, would turn into ammonia.

Smoke was still heavy on the field, drifting from the Mark 89 Raider down upon the attacker. It was impossible to see what this unexpected enemy was about but an occasional clang said that his doors were open.

On a very high trajectory, butt to earth, the converted riot gun began to fire. It made no explosion. It hissed no louder than an ammunition belt that might be caught in the burning shack. But the jet went up above the smoke and it came down into the drift from the burning space vessel.

Kit let it spray until he had but a quarter of a gun left. Then he throttled it off.

"Cover me," he said to Young, handing him the tool box.

He ran forward, crouching low, fitting an atmosphere mask to his face as he went, and shortly came into cleared space through which the attacker's bulk loomed greyly.

He half expected a shot but none came.

He need not have worried.

Four crewmen were outside the space ship, rolling on the ground in agony, clawing at their faces and chests until blood flowed.

They did not even see Kit. He went up the ladder to the open port and turned the gun inside. He let it go for half its remaining charge and then followed up in person.

Ship officers, quartermasters, tubemen, all in that shining, undamaged interior, were blind with the terrible fury of drifting ammonia clouds. The newest charge made a gunner scream in last agony and fall senseless at Kit's feet.

Kit thrust his mask into every compartment before he would trust the ship and ther he began to pile disarmed men outside by dropping them through the ports and turrets.

Young struggled to get near, retired and put on a mask and then came up to help. In a very short time they had the people who had been flung around the outside of the ship piled into a neat stack which one man with a gun could command.

Several were dead, some were hardly affected beyond temporary blindness. Kit dropped one last tube-man down the steps, booted him into the pile and then began to fish about amongst the arms, legs and torsos. He dragged out a tweed pants leg and had the man spread before him. The papers in his pocket said that he was "Jacklin Arl, Universal Uranium." That was all Kit wanted to know.

Henry was there, coughing and staying outside the range in a response to Kit's yell. "Who's that? Who's calling?"

"It's me, Kit! Who is alive?"

"Larsen and me got Sailor out. He's wounded. Everybody is dead. . . . It's really you,

Kit?" He coughed in the smoke and backed away.

Kit appeared like a devil from a caldron and Henry blinked. "It is you. Then you whipped that ship. . . ." There was awe in Henry's voice. He turned and sprinted back to tell Sailor and to give him aid.

Chapter Twelve

TWENTY MINUTES LATER KIT HAD THE SHIP blown out, three volunteers from the survivors sworn to everlasting loyalty and somewhat recovered from ammonia—enough at least to man their stations—and was ready to take off.

Henry and Larsen got the wounded Sailor into a berth where Henry gave him medical aid.

"What happened?" begged Sailor Ah Wing faintly.

"It's that Kit," said Henry. "Whooee! What a boy that Kit is! Don't monkey with him any because he's a hurricane on a rampage, yes sir! Take a sip of this, now. Your burns will heal fast enough."

"Where's that general what's-his-name?" said Sailor.

"The last I seen of him, he was a curled up cap ornament," said Henry. "There's the phone to the bridge. I got to go."

"Go? Are we going someplace?" said Sailor.

"The devil knows! But that's a 'Stand-by' gong you hear ringing and that Kit is one mad redhead. He says 'Go,' we got to go."

"But Vanpoll . . . orders?"

"Sailor, we seem to be taking orders from that Kit and me for one don't mind at all, at all."

Henry reached the bridge of the big cruiser and blinked at the controls and telegraphs and visoplates. He stepped into the gymbals of the pilot's chair and gingerly put his big hand on the keyboard control system. It was standard, anyway.

This high in the ship he could look out across the town where the red light of Darengo played weirdly upon the billowing clouds of smoke. The place looked like the last stages of doom and Henry shuddered.

"Wooee, that Kit!" he said.

That Kit was issuing out of the crumbling remains of the Raider which he had checked in vain for any survivor. He stood for a moment looking at the town and then at the heavens. He turned then and sprinted for the big cruiser.

Somewhere below Henry heard a door bang and the keepers thud home. Fuel feeders began to whine as they warmed up. There were metal boots clanging on ladder rungs and a stream of reports in the intercommunicator.

Kit's hand was solid on Henry's shoulder. "All firing?"

"All firing, sir."

"Hull tight?"

"Hull tight, sir," said Henry.

"Shift gravity, rise to four thousand feet and stand by. Switch on all lookouts. Young! Scan the screens here."

Young sank into the watch officer's red morocco chair and mopped his face with a red bandana. "Oh, my Lord. I'm a ruin. Where's the water up here? I'll never get rid of that ammonia."

"You better watch those guard screens," said Henry, "if Kit says so."

Young nodded and revived. He was suddenly aware of very angry voices in the chart room just behind them.

And Jacklin Arl, with all the bluster at his command, pride as well as body stung by that ammonia, was trying to give Kit a bad time.

"You'll get nothing from me," he snarled. "Your accusation is preposterous. We had no interest in Saint Martin. We. . . ."

Kit slapped his face and the sneer vanished. Arl got up unsteadily. He was impressed with the fury in this flame-tipped man.

"Wreck a planet will you? Attack it with all the scum of space, will you? Murder and rape and burn, will you?"

The crack of the second slap was loud and Arl went down again. "It isn't me, it's the company. I just work for the company. I tell you I don't know."

Kit looked at the sharp, dark face with disgust. The evil, twitching eyes could not stand to his and Arl sagged down. Kit yanked him to his feet and slapped him flat again.

"Tell me where the Arbiter can be found. Tell me now and tell me fast!"

"I've nothing to do with him!" wailed Arl. "We are no part of him. For Messiah's sake, don't hit me again."

"I'd love to beat you to jelly," said Kit. "In fact, I think I will! Murderer! Filthy carrion! Wreck a planet, will you. . . ." Smack!

"If . . . if I tell you where to find the Arbiter, will you stop?"

Kit stood back, breathing hard, not because of exertion but because of fury. "Talk."

"Terra. He's on Terra. We know where he is. Zone of Hawaii, Terra. The whole defense of it is for the Arbitration Council. The Arbiter. . . . Say! You're not going there? You're not going to attack him? Not the Arbiter! With me on board. . . . Not the Arbiter and his ship-screens. You'll never live through it. Never."

"You'd better be sure you are right," said Kit. And then he stood looking at the man that groveled at his space boots and became convinced. "Take-off!" he yelled to Henry.

The big cruiser leaped up to four thousand feet and poised there, scanners going.

"What's that?" said Henry, staring at the ground screen.

Young looked. The picture, moving as the scanner swept, showed a town bounded by a sea on one side and a quiet, topsy-turvy line of dead men on the other. They lay in a circular pattern, very precise, and there must have been eight thousand of them. The outlying fringe was ragged where some had tried to crawl away before they died. And over this grisly scene, painted red by Darengo, drifted palls of smoke.

Young blanched but his voice was firm. "Batille's troops. They came back on the run from wherever they were, landed their carriers outside and swarmed in to investigate the explosions and smoke. They found the force screen gone because we destroyed it. And they marched through the invisible quarter-centimeter radar barrier and got fried to a man before they knew it." His tone was dead as he saw the result of their first operation.

"Kit did that? Wooee! It's an army dead."

"Scum of space," said Kit. "The civilians can take over now and mop up the units that remain. Look, Young. See that sub-station there. That's the key. Drop me a missile on it keyed to the dynatrodes."

Young hurriedly rose and went aft. Kit stared at the scanner. "It's not a nice sight, Henry. But some things have to be done. Bar sweepings. I don't think they'll be missed. No decent man would have made himself a part of that army."

There was a flash on the screen and the sub-station disintegrated. The pieces of radar equipment and masonry floated softly back and left their smoke added to that of the town.

"That's the end of the barrier," said Kit. "They can take care of themselves down there now. Reverse yesterday's course." He took down the intercommunicator mike. "Stand by fore and aft. Seven *g's* Duration of flight eight days. Signal when ready."

"Ready," said the starboard tubes.

"Ready," said the port tubes.

"Ready," said the steering tubes.

"Ready," said the fuel room.

Henry nodded and poised his hand over the keyboard, the cruiser swinging to his course.

"Cruiser! Take-off!"

Flame and quivering thunderbolts of power, plumes of fire in the blue. The cruiser sped for Terra, Zone of Hawaii.

Chapter Thirteen

Lancing through the ink of space, past comet and dying star, Christopher Randolph Kellan applied himself to his plans. The rage which had burned in him was like the forge fire which makes steel; the impurities were scorched from him in his headlong crusade to rid the universe, as he told Henry, "of a rotten cancer that will eat through a million years of man's hoarded gains of culture and leave him naked and defenseless, all to appease the greed of one man."

If he had not been so intent upon his studies and plans he might have recalled that any *agente saboteur* must guard against treachery in his crew. After all, what did he know of some of these men he trusted?

He might have recalled how the communication webs of space are held. Each system, using its outermost planet because of its slower rotation, maintained a threaded "wire" connecting to central systems which in turn could relay anything by way of communicaion anywhere. The "wire" consisted of ionized beaming and was constantly fed outwards. Laid originally by space ships going five or six hundred times the speed of light, and so used that impulses could reach down them almost instantaneously, the communication problem of space (anything traveling the speed of light would ordinarily take tens, hundreds or even thousands of years even as the starlight travels) had been for some two hundred years solved. Across and near many web stations the cruiser must inevitably go, despite the "tracklessness" of space.

If he had not been so intent in the fifteenth watch of the voyage, he might have heard the small clicks of an outer space instrument telling off the words in the communication room just behind him. He might have heard the stealthy whisper of a door being opened and shut and the small clink of a keybolt dropping; or the sibilance of bare feet on the passage deck might have told him that honest men would wear space boots against the cold. But he was deep in his charts and that was the important thing, of course.

Drinking hot coffee to stay awake, he learned that he was perilously embarked. The cruiser's chartroom was extraordinarily well fitted with charts and pilots. These were carried on small slides of practically no weight so that their aggregate millions would not weigh more than a kilo. They shone upon a luminescent screen which could be pencil marked and scrubbed clean again, and their manufacture and projection was an intricate thing which reduced all aberration to naught. The star and planet pilots were on reels of wire, a page to the micro-inch, and screened similarly beside the charts.

It was amazing to him how little he actually knew of Terra when all was said. He could quote whole chapters from star pilots, but the simple wordage of the Terra Hydrographic Office pilots, having to do with mountains and rivers and seas which he had seen and never labeled for an instant of a swift descent, were entirely new to him.

He found the Zone of Hawaii. He found a great deal about soundings in the "Pacific Ocean" around it and about sea currents and storms and the general atmosphere. But each time he would come close to something which would help him it would be labeled "Censored."

Indeed there was something peculiar about the Zone of Hawaii. It was a cone of non-approach to all incoming craft. It was a signal station which would not communicate. It was a "defended area." And for all he could tell it must be bristling with large red signs which told people to stay away and keep away or get their jolly heads shot off.

He gave up being adroit and then he gave up being bull-headed. He recalled finally that any space ship cares very little about water and remembered the take-off of the Mark 89 Raider.

Thus it was, one bright sunshiny afternoon that a certain cruiser was picked up by the

Earth scans, came through the intercept bands at a dangerous speed and was reported crashed in the Pacific in the region of Canton Island. And thus it was that the rescue craft which went there immediately found no trace.

Men at their stations, prisoner locked in tight, tubes off and landing treads whirring, the big vessel plowed fifty fathoms deep through the calm, calm Pacific at a hundred miles an hour.

Henry and the Chinese stood on either side of the control keyboard, water green against the "fish-bowl" and had very little to say.

"Vanpoll will not like this," ventured the Sailor at last.

Henry did not reply.

"This is pretty dangerous," said Sailor.

The hand on the keyboard did not shake.

"We had better land with him," said Sailor.

Henry jerked his head in a brief nod.

The sun went down and the cruiser crept on all night. At four o'clock, two hours before daybreak, she was lying to on the crests of easy swells, cool moist air blowing into her long-sealed interior.

Young and Henry were wrestling with a space lifeboat which had jammed in its ejectors. The starlight was all they had. Kit would not allow heat sources of any kind to be used. From time to time Young would bark his knuckles or shins and swear. Kit was playing a night glass over the bold outlines of Diamond Head, trying to find anything which would suggest buildings. He had just noticed, well to his left, that a cluster of lights made a

110

glow over the sea rim and he took a hasty check on the course to them.

The space lifeboat grated free and Henry jumped into it, holding it off the hull with a gun butt.

Kit climbed down into the boat as it fell and raised alongside and was suprised to find Sailor Ah Wing on his heels.

"Get back. Young and I. . . ."

"We are going with you," said Henry. "Let Young look to the ship."

Kit did not like it but Sailor Ah Wing and Henry were determined. Kit finally turned to the deck. "Young. Submerge her and stand off until dark tonight, same place. "Take her away from us."

Hatches closed, there was a whirr of tractors and the big ship drove steadily and smoothly out of sight. Kit pulled on the dome of the lifeboat and started to take his place at the controls.

Ah Wing's voice was very cold. "Keep your hands away from your gun, Kellan. Up, that's it." He started to take Kit's sidearm and Kit whirled savagely to strike.

A blow which dented his helmet took him solidly. He dropped to his knees. The boat rocked. He tried hard to get up but his wrists were turned to jelly and would not support him. The rocking of the boat turned into a steady, dark spin with a red core and then he knew nothing.

Chapter Fourteen

GUARDS HAD HIM BY EACH ARM AND IT SUR-
prised him that the morning sun was so high.
He braced his feet and tried to wrench free
but the guards were not to be denied. Sun
blazed down on their golden corselets where a
scale of justice was engraved. "Equity for All.
Galactic Arbitration Council." Kit felt sick and
the sunlight hurt his eyes. The fountain by
which they dragged him was wickedly plaintive, mocking him with its coolness.

"You might let me take a drink," he pleaded.

One of the guards, tall and blond, shoved
him to the fountain's rim. There was much to
be learned from the sureness with which he
acted. Out past the gates were invisible cordons
and traps no man could negotiate without intricate knowledge. Overhead were disintegrator
cones through which no plane, ship or bomb
could penetrate intact. In watchtowers on the

courtyard walls were guards behind long-snouted weapons. The very pavement was copper which could carry a killing jolt at the single depression of a button.

The palms knocked quietly against the side of the building wall. A wide verandah, set about with easy wicker chairs, provided shade. They dragged Kit through the inner door and into a huge hall. A fountain was playing here, presided over by four golden nymphs who forever regarded their own reflections and smiled. The wind rustled tapestry and made it flash with its gold thread and precious-stoned border.

Where was Henry? What had Ah Wing. . . . And not until then did he remember. Henry must be dead and Ah Wing had sold out to the enemy.

The guards shoved him into a chair and the tall blond one went inside a large chamber. Voices rumbled in there for a long time and then there was a scraping of chairs and two old men came forth, napkins in hand, to look briefly, even amusedly at Kit and walk on to some other part of the building.

The tall blond one came back and beckoned. Kit was forced to his feet and shoved into the room.

A very old man in a white cap was sitting at the head of half an acre of dining table. Six places had been set besides his but they were all empty. The chairs were high-backed and massive. Brocade stirred on either side of the great windows. A pool of sunlight fell about the very old man.

"This is he," said the tall, blond guard.

The ancient one nodded. "Be seated, if you please. I wish to have conversation with you." He was quite courteous. "Have you breakfasted?"

"Hardly," said Kit. "But I am not hungry." He sat down and a soft-footed servant girl laid an orange on a plate before him. The tall blond guard ostentatiously cleared away all cutlery from Kit's reach.

"You seem to have been very busy," said the old man, looking at a sheaf of paper which lay among the silver and crystal remains of his breakfast.

"If you want me to talk, I'm afraid. . . ."

"There's not much occasion for it," said the old man. "I have it all here. Hmmm. Still, it doesn't say what you did, precisely, on Saint Martin. Seem to have cleared the matter up. This is all a little premature, you know."

"I have my opinion of wrecking planets," said Kit solidly, ire beginning to rise.

"Now, now," said the old man. "Quietly, quietly, please. Suppose you tell me exactly what you did. Your man Young was very reticent."

"Young?" gasped Kit.

"Of course. We took the cruiser shortly after you left her and have the people all safe. This Jacklin Arl. . . ."

He stopped and looked at a door far down the room. "Have Mr. Carlyle in here."

Kit sagged. He would be completely identified now.

Carlyle came, very deferential. He nodded to

to the old man and then looked closely at Kit. Carlyle nodded again with certainty and withdrew.

"Have Jacklin Arl in," said the old man.

They brought him, fuming and complaining. He glared at the old man and at Kit. "Yes," he raged, "this is the fellow on Saint Martin. He did us up proper, too."

They took Arl out.

"We weren't quite sure. In fact, I'll have to ask. . . ." He made a motion and the tall blond guard took off Kit's helmet. Then he produced a piece of glass wrapped in a paper, rolled out some bromo ink and took a quick set of prints from Kit. He went out and came back in a moment. "This is undoubtedly the same young man, sir."

The thoroughness of it was beginning to get Kit.

"You will not tell me the names of your associates."

"No," said Kit. "I will not. You will learn nothing from me, no matter what you use."

The old man's brows shot up. "Hold him outside and summon the council," he said.

Kit fretted at the door. He could hear the buzzing voices, several raised in loud argument, several shouting them down all at once. It was like the sea ebbing and flowing and Kit's head ached terribly. He wondered what kind of executions they did. Probably they were debating whether to boil him in oil or pull him apart with wild horses. And still the conference went on.

A servant brought Kit a glass of something

and he was afraid to touch it until she sipped from it first. Then he drank it down and his headache vanished. Strength began to flow into him from the slightly bitter fluid.

The doors sprang open and a crowd came out. They were of all sizes and modes of dress and they were still debating with one another. One or two looked curiously at Kit. He could make nothing of their conversation for many were toothless and all were old. The flow swept on into a larger chamber across the hall and then the doors shut.

Kit waited. After some time a messenger came out and the guards yanked Kit to his feet. They propelled him forward under a great black arch and into a marble-floored hall large enough for a ball.

At one end was a high desk, of solid gold against a mural of the galaxy idealized by pictures of man's efforts. There sat the old man with whom he had talked. The seats, arranged semi-circularly about the bench, were deep and soft and the audience was nearly sunk from sight. Kit was shoved down to the front and up on a stand.

"Your name?" said the old man.

"Christopher Randolph Kellan."

"Your age?"

"Thirty."

"Mr. Kellan, correct me if I am wrong." And the old man read, in a high old man's voice, a precise account of every instant of importance in Kit's entire life. He came to the space roving between the years of school and there were things in it which Kit did not know that anyone in the universe would ever find out. He came to the tempestuous college career and there were even Kit's abominable grades. He came to the matters of the P.R.S. and finally read, at greater length than the rest, of Kit's rage against anyone who would wreck a planet.

That done, at long last, the old man laid the paper down. He changed his glasses and looked at the assembled.

"If anyone now has a dissenting voice, let that be heard."

There was silence.

"If anyone disagrees or refuses in any particular, let him speak," said the old man.

There was not one voice and Kit's heart dropped. None to defend him. Not one!

The old man then rose and took off the soft white cap with its gold-embroidered scales. He took off the white robe and he removed the six seal rings.

"He's going to do it himself," shuddered Kit.

But if the old man contemplated violence, it was not in his face. "Step up here."

Kit dazedly stepped up.

The old man put his hands on Kit's shoulders. "Your hair is very red, even as mine used to be. But you favor your mother."

Kit couldn't record it in his wits.

"You are tall and strong. I was once," said the old man with a quiet smile. "And in you, I am again. Gentlemen of the Council, ministers and ambassadors of the galaxy, I present to you my son! Christopher Randolph Kellan Marshal!"

Councilmen, ambassadors, ministers, envoys

and messengers and even the guards at the door loosed off a cheer which made the roofbeams tremble and stood, pressing forward.

"Please, gentlemen," said the Arbiter, "you will be presented individually one at a time. But a moment of silence please while I acquaint my puzzled son with facts withheld from him until now."

The Arbiter turned to Kit. "You are my son. Later I can tell you many things and ask your pardon for this sudden storming of your brains. But before you judge me harshly for the fate to which I consigned you so long ago, please listen to my argument.

"When you were born, the doctors said you would be strong and brilliant and before you were one they had proven you as genius by their tests.

"I was faced then with a future problem. The post of aribter I had won by might and strength because of the fear which was in man. But as time progressed it was obvious to me that I would have no chance to raise a son as he should be raised. For these and such as these would fawn and turn your head with sycophancy. The world would be an unreal association with great names and nations and these, I fear, would have bent you into unseemly patterns of thought. This was no place to raise a son. In those days we were not so safe as now and as you would have been a target for deadly sycophancy, so would you have been an object of kidnap and murder.

"You must be trained, I thought, and you must know the little peoples of the worlds among the stars. You must be strong and self reliant. And in case I died you must be informed and given a choice as to what your own career would be.

"Your 'Aunt Isabel' is your mother, unhappy woman denied to me through all these cares of state. She knew how close you were to death as Marshal and it was partly her choice to raise you Kellan, my mother's name.

"You were trained then as no school in all the security-frightened systems would have trained you. Some of the men you have called 'Professor Jones' or 'Instructor Smith' have been the greatest scientists in all the galaxy. And I made your mother break the tedium of study by sending you to far places with positions amongst the little people of space so that you would know and understand them and know why man progresses—for he goes forward as an individual only and not all the great governments and companies in the universe can be aught without that single individual, the ordinary man. And as he is happy and free, so do they prosper and not otherwise. But this you know."

The Arbiter looked at the sea of white faces.

"When your apprenticeship was done and you knew the worlds of space, their machines, their philosophies and their frailties, you were to come here. But there were those amongst these men who objected. They said you would have no love of man, that you might be unserious and unfitted."

Loud cries of "No! No!" from the whole chamber.

"They said you were without experience," continued the Arbiter. "They said we were grown old and that space was in sorry state and that a sure and vengeful hand was needed in this place. But that you could not be fitted to be that hand. And so we arranged to make a trial of you. Oh, the conferences there have been in this hall upon the subject of one redheaded boy, wandering out in the spaceways and all unwitting of his fate! And I struck upon a mechanism to prove you, not to me, but to them, for they were doubtful and afraid."

"No! No!" flooded up again but the old man gave no heed.

"Using Vanpoll there . . ." and here Kit gaped at Peter Vanpoll who was smiling at him not five feet away, ". . . and one of our subsidiary infiltration organizations, the People's Revolutionary Society, we withdrew all records of you from your schools and so made your university suspicious. Then Sikes here . . ." and Kit gaped again for there was the S.B.I. man who should have been stone dead, ". . . was 'killed' so that you could be trapped as one of their kingslayers, for I regret to say that assassination is also a political weapon.

"You had heard the name of Arbiter hardly used for we were failing and wars and commercially stimulated revolts were becoming common things, almost beyond our control, palsied with age as we are. And so with my butler they call Sailor Ah Wing and Henry my chauffeur to guarantee, we hoped, you would not be killed, you were sent out. But Vanpoll fumbled

120

and you went alone and met Carlyle who knew nothing of you. I think you angered him by beating him at chess or some such thing. . . ."

Carlyle, across the room, shuffled uncomfortably.

"Carlyle," continued the Arbiter, "as a lesser agent, was eager to catch you and sent your description throughout space. What trouble we had quashing that! But you stole the machine of war which we now have along with your man Young and so concluded your first case. There were supposed to have been seven in all before you were sent here.

"But fate has a special sauce for red hair, it seems. You solved a riddle on Saint Martin which had baffled us for eighteen months. We did not know that Universal Uranium, which we had trusted well, was at the root of that. And we were old and used diplomacy instead of force which won the galaxy's peace throughout our youth. I shudder at the dangers you ran. For you went entirely out of hand and leaped to conclusions from which you had no escape. You settled the business handsomely and when these gentlemen here heard what you did and how, they cheered you to the echoes and when our Henry sent us word you were even going to attack us and why you'd made the error, they could not wait to greet you when you came. For they know we are failing and they know we need new strength.

"A little while ago they forced my hand. You were to be here six months to observe us and to study our networks of organizations for control and the prevention of war and economic set-backs—which you must know by now are caused by man himself, not us. But I say they forced my hand. They read all these lengthy reports upon your entire life and heard your deeds with open mouths and then they demanded that I do this thing that I do now, and believe me, my son, it is with pride that I can.

"Christoper Randolph Kellan Marshal, will you take the charge of maintaining equity in all space and forwarding the purposes and organizations of the Galactic Arbitration Council?"

Kit stared at him. "Take . . . what?"

"I am old, Christopher. I have waited all your life for this. Do you accept?"

Kit found himself in the robe, found the seals on his fingers and the cap on his head and stood, buffeted by the cheering crowd, looking dazedly down at himself. Lines were forming to greet him and shake his hand and his father, his very own father that he had wished for for so long was standing there to help him.

Somewhere back in the room Sailor Ah Wing was grinning and Henry was saying over and over, "Just like his daddy looked when he took office. Just like him. I remember. Just like his daddy!" And he was bursting with pride so that his chauffeur's buttons creaked.

Young, far back, rested himself in an ambassador's chair. He was trembling, he had been so afraid for his "general." But soon Kit would come and tell him what to do and there'd be days of hectic building and planning in some wonderfully God-forsaken outpost of space and governments would change and fall and new ones would rise. He steadied his nervous hands and bided himself to wait.

Only Peter Vanpoll was worried. He edged forward to speak to the old man. Carlyle was offering Kit a hand through the jostling throng. "Know you'll find it a frightful bore, old boy. But shah matte, eh? shah matte!"

Vanpoll whispered to old Mr. Marshal and there was worry in it.

"You were especially instructed . . ." began the old man. But he was too choked up with joy to be very angry. "Who is she?"

Vanpoll whispered, "Bright and pretty. I promise you she never knew his destiny. Truly she was not trading on that."

"Then have her in," said the old man. "Have her in."

And Carla came through the great black doors, frightened at the crowd and dazed to see her man up there, but pretty in her fright and deferred to on every hand. Kit stopped in mid-greeting and stared.

"Carla!" he cried and sprang forward to her side. And then it was all real to him and all true. He showed her the robe and the gavel and the small gold scales of office and the blazing seals on the rings. And she touched them and smiled at him and Kit all in a flurry introduced her to his father.

"This is jet and . . . I mean this is Carla, Father."

The old man beamed upon her. His son had fully as good taste on women as himself. And Carla, the bold Carla, bowed shyly to him and quickly took Kit's arm.

"My future daughter-in-law, gentlemen," said the old man to the ambassadors and ministers, envoys and messengers.

They cheered her. They cheered Kit. They cheered the Council and the old man. They cheered the galaxy and then they cheered Carla and Kit again all over.

And down in the prison under the great hall, Jacklin Arl shuddered, shuddered like all tyranny and greed would shudder under the reign of the new Arbiter who, in his young and competent hands held the fate and destiny of all governments in space from one rim of the galaxy to the other.

A gentle Pacific breeze through the window gently worked upon the symbolic scales of the bench, one side of which was down. Slowly, quietly, the upper pan dropped low and the lower pan came up until they balanced there, steady and serene.

The Beast

THE CRASH AND THE SCREAM WHICH REVER-
berated through the stinking gloom of the
Venusian night brought Ginger Cranston to a
startled halt upon the trail, held there for an
instant by the swirl of panicked blues which
made up the *safari* of the white hunter.

Something had happened to the head of the
line, something sudden, inexplicable in this
foggy blackness.

Ginger Cranston did not long remain motionless for the blues had dumped their packages
and had vanished, leaving the narrow trail,
which wandered aimlessly through the giant
trees, clear of men.

He took one step forward, gun balanced at
the ready in the crook of his arm and then the
thing happened to him which would make his
life a nightmare.

From above and behind something struck

him, struck him with a fury and a savageness which sent him flat into the muck, which began to claw and rake and beat at him with a singleness of intent which would have no ending short of death.

The white hunter rolled in the slime and beat back with futile fists, kicking out with his heavy boots, smothering under the gagging odor of a wild animal, so strong that it penetrated through the filters of his swamp mask, the only thing which was saving his face from the sabers this thing had for claws.

Fighting it back, the hunter's hands could find no grip upon the slimy fur; he could see nothing of it because of the dark and the fact that the blues had dropped their torches to a man. Ginger luridly cursed the blues, cursed this thing, cursed the muck and the agony which was being hammered into him.

He lurched to his knees, striking out blindly with all his might. The thing was driven back from him for an instant and Ginger's hands raked the mud around him for some weapon, preferably his lost gun. When he could not find it he leaped all the way to his feet and ripped away the swamp mask. He could not see. He could hear the snarling grunts of the thing as it gathered itself for a second charge.

Something in the unexpectedness of the attack, something in the ferocity of the beast, shook Ginger's courage, a courage which was a byword where hunters gathered. For a moment he could think of nothing but trying to escape this death which would again be upon him in an instant. He whirled and fumbled his

126

way through the trees. If he could find some place where he could make a stand, if he could grasp a precious instant to get out and unclasp his knife—

There was a roaring sound hard by, the sound of battered water. Ginger knew this continent better than to go so far off a trail and he knew he must here make that stand. He gathered his courage about him like armor. He unclasped the knife. He could feel the beast not two yards away from him but in the dense gloom he could not see anything but the vague shapes of trees.

It struck. It struck from behind with a strength which brought them crashing into the mud and branches. One cruel paw was crooked to feel out with its sabers the eyes of its victim, the others scored Ginger's back and side.

Rolling in a red agony, strong beyond any past strength, Ginger tried to slam his assailant back against a tree. He could not grip the slimy, elusive paw but he could brace it away from him with his forearm.

A roaring sound was loud in Ginger's ears and before he could halt the last roll he had managed, beast and hunter were over the lip and into black and greedy space. A shattering cry came from the beast as it fell away.

Ginger tried to see, tried to twist in the air and then he was gagged by the thick sirup of the depths and twisted like a chip in the strength of a whirlpool. He struck upward and then could not orient himself. His lungs began to burn and the sirup of the river seared his throat. The whirlpool flung him out, battered him against a rock and then left him to crawl, stunned and aching, from the stream.

He lay on the rocks, deafened by the roar of the water, trying to find strength enough to scan the space around him in search of the beast.

Two hours later the frightened blues, grouped in a hollow ring for security, found the white hunter by the river and placed him in a sling. One of the trackers nervously examined a nearby track and then cried, "Da juju! Da juju!" Hastily the carriers lifted the sling and bore its inert burden back to the trail and along it to the village which had been Ginger Cranston's goal.

Ginger Cranston woke slowly into the oppressive odor of a blue village from the tangled terror of his dreams. The heated ink of the Venusian night eddied through his tent, clung clammily to his face, smothered the native fires which burned across the clearing. Ginger Cranston woke into a new sensation, a feeling of loss, and for a little while could not bring organization into thought. It was hard for him to bring back the successive shocks which had placed him here, helpless in this bed, and he began to know things which it had never before occurred to him that it would be important to know.

He had always been a brave man. As government hunter of this continent, relentlessly wiping out the ponderous and stupid game which threatened the settlements and their crops, he had been considered all about as a man without peer in the lists of courage. So certain had he been in his possession of this confidence that he had never wondered about fear, had found only contempt for those who were so weak as to feel that lowly emotion.

And now Ginger Cranston woke up afraid.

The shocks, wreaked upon another, would have brought madness. To have been struck twice from behind by a raging beast, to have tasted death between the claws of such fury, would have wrecked the usual nervous system. But Ginger Cranston was not a usual person and, never having been other than his gay, confident self, he had no standards.

He had lost his courage.

In its place was a sick nausea.

And Ginger Cranston, out of shame, was no help to himself but stood away from his battered body and gazed with lip-curled contempt upon this sniveling hulk which stood at the brink of recalling that which had brought this about. He had no sympathy for himself and had no reasons with which to excuse his state.

He was ill and his spirits, as in anyone ill, were low. He had been expecting the same stupid, many-tonned brutes which he had thought to constitute the only game of this continent. He had been set upon by a thing wholly unknown to him at a time when he had expected nothing and he had been mauled badly in the process. But he offered himself none of these. He was afraid, afraid of an unknown, cunning something, the memory of which was real in this dark tent.

"Ambu!" he yelled.

A Venusian of wary step and worried eyes

slunk into the tent. Ambu had done his bungling best with these wounds, hurling the offer of help back into the teeth of the village doctor —a person who prefered a ghost rattle to a bottle of iodine. Ambu was of uncertain age, uncertain bearing. He was half in and half out of two worlds—that of the whites in Yorkville on the coast, that of the blues in the somber depths of this continent. He believed in ghosts. But he knew that iodine prevented infection. He belonged to a white, had been indifferently schooled by the whites. But he was a blue.

Ambu hung the lanter on the pole of the tent and looked uneasily at his white man. He was not encouraged by that strange expression in the hunter's eyes, but the fact that Lord Ginger had come back to consciousness was cheering.

Ginger was feeling a strange relief at having light. He smiled unconvincingly. When he spoke his voice was carefully controlled.

"Well, Ambu! I'm not dead yet, you see."

"Ambu is very happy, Lord Ginger." He looked worried.

"What . . . er . . . what happened out there when . . . well, what happened?" said Ginger with another smile.

Ambu looked into the dark corners of the tent, looked out into the compound and then sank on his dull haunches at the side of the cot.

"Devils," said Ambu.

"Nonsense," said Ginger in careful carelessness.

"Devils," said Ambu. "There was a pit. I have never before seen such a pit. It was dug

130

deep with claw marks on the digging. It was covered over with branches and mud like a roof; when the trackers stepped upon it they fell through. There were sharpened stakes at the bottom to receive them. They do not live, Lord Ginger."

"A deadfall?" gasped Ginger. And then, because there was a resulting emotion which clamored to be felt, he spoke swiftly, carelessly, and smothered it. "Nonsense. There's nothing like a deadfall in the arts of the blues. There have been no hostile blues for thirty years or more."

"Devils," said Ambu. "Devils of the dark, not blues. I have never seen nor heard of such a trap, Lord Ginger."

"I'll have to see it before I believe it," said Ginger. "Er . . . Ambu, bring me a drink."

Ambu was perceptive. He knew Lord Ginger did not mean water even though Lord Ginger never drank except to be polite or when ill with fever. He poured from a flat metal bottle into a metal cup and the two chattered together.

"Very cold tonight," said Ambu, sweating.

"Very cold," said Ginger, drinking quickly.

The beasts of this continent weighed many tons. They were of many kinds, some of them carnivorous, all of them stupid, slothful swamp creatures which did damage because they were clumsy not because they were vicious. It was a government hunter's job to kill them because a man had to be skilled to rend apart enough flesh and muscle and bone to keep the brutes from traveling. There were no small animals like leopards or lynxes. On all Venus there was nothing which weighed four hundred pounds and had claws, was cloaked in slimy fur—

"It *knew*," said Ambu. "It knew Lord Ginger would stop in just that place when the line halted. And it was on a tree limb above Lord Ginger waiting for him to stop. It *knew*."

"Rot and nonsense," grinned Ginger carefully. "I have never heard of a beast with that much intelligence."

"No beast," said Ambu with rare conviction for him. "Probably devil. No doubt devil. Forest devil. Drink again, Lord Ginger?"

Ginger drank again and some of the numb horror began to retreat before the warmth of the liquor. "Well, maybe we'll take a crack at hunting it when we've disposed of this "juju" thing the village is troubled about."

"The devil is 'da juju'," said Ambu. "That is the thing for which they wanted Lord Ginger. That was 'da juju'!"

"The white lord is well?" said a new voice, a tired and hopeless voice, in the entrance to the tent.

Ambu started up guiltily and began to protest to the chief in blue that the white lord was well enough but would talk to no one.

"Never mind, Ambu. Invite him in," said Ginger. He knew he would get the full impact of this thing now, would remember all about it, would receive the hopelessness of this gloomy forest chief like one receives an immersion in ink. "Greetings," said Ginger in blue.

"Greetings to the white lord," said the chief tiredly. "He lives and the village Tohyvo is happy that he lives. The white hunter is great and his fame is mighty. He comes and all things flee in horror before him. The blues beat their heads against the earth in submission and hide their eyes before the dazzling brilliance of the mighty lord." He sighed and sank upon an ammunition box.

"Greetings to the star of his people," said Ginger, mechanically. "His name carries the storm of his wrath across the jungle and his power is as the raging torrent. A flash of his glance is the lightning across the storm." He took a cup of liquor from Ambu and handed it to the dispirited, sodden little chief.

"You met da juju," said the chief.

"We did," said Ginger with a timed smile. "On the next meeting da juju will be dead."

"Ah," said the chief.

"You have had some trouble with this thing?" said Ginger.

"My best warriors are gutted and mangled corpses in the forest depths. Women going to the river have never returned. Children are snatched from play. And always the dark swallows this thing, always there is only the silent forest to mock. In my long life I have never heard of such a beast. But you have said it will be killed. It is good. It is ended. The mighty hunter gives me back my sleep."

"Wait," said Ginger. "You say it makes raids on your village?"

"Yes, mighty warrior."

"How does it do this?"

"It rides down from the sky. It vanishes back into the sky."

"You mean the trees," said Ginger.

"It is the same," sighed the chief, eyeing the liquor bottle.

"How do your warriors die?"

The chief squirmed. "They fall into pits cunningly placed on the trail and covered over. They are attacked from behind and torn to bits. Da juju has even been known to wrest from their hands their spears and knives and transfix them with their own weapons."

Ambu was shivering. He stood on one foot, then on the other. He scratched his back nervously and in the next second scratched his head. His eyes, flicking back and forth from the chief to the white hunter were like a prisoner's under torture.

"Maybe devils," said Ambu.

"Devils," muttered the old chief. "The mighty white warrior has come. All will be well. All will be well." He looked dispiritedly at Ginger and crept out of the tent.

Ambu pointed to a case which contained a radiophone. "Lord Ginger talk Yorkville and ask for men?"

Ginger startled himself by almost agreeing. He had never asked for help. He was Ginger Cranston. He looked at the radio case like a desert-stranded man might gaze thirstily at a cup of water before he did the incredible thing of pouring it out on the ground.

"We won't need any help," said Ginger with a smile. "All I need is a night's sleep. Have the chief throw out beaters in the morning and pick up the beast's track. Meantime, good night. NO!" he added quickly and then calmed

134

his voice. "No, leave the lantern there, Ambu. I . . . I have some notes to make."

Ambu looked uncertainly at his white master and then sidled from the tent.

The giant trees stood an infinity into the sky, tops lost in the gray dark of swirling vapors. Great tendrils of fog crept ghostily, low past the trunks, to blot with their evil odor of sulphur and rot what visibility the faint light might have permitted. It was an atmosphere in which men unconsciously speak in whispers and look cautiously around each bend before venturing farther along the trail.

The beaters had come back with news that da juju had left tracks in a clearing two kilometers from the village and they added to it the usual blue exaggeration that it was certain da juju was wounded from his encounter with the mighty white hunter.

The party stepped cautiously past an open space where some wrecked and forgotten space liner, which furnished the natives with metal, showed a series of battered ports through the swirling gloom, a ship to be avoided since its dryness offered refuge to snakes.

Weak and feverish, Ginger occasionally stopped and leaned against a tree. He would have liked the help of Ambu's arm, but could not, in his present agitated state, bring himself to ask for it.

Step by step, turn by turn of the trail, a thing was growing inside Ginger Cranston, a thing which was like a lash upon his nerves. His back was slashed with the wounds he had received and the wounds burned, burned with memory.

His back was cringing away from the thing it had experienced and as the minutes went the feeling increased. At each or any instant he expected to have upon him once again the shock of attack, from behind, fraught with agony and terror. He tired to sweep it from him. He tried to reassure himself by inspecting the low-hanging limbs under which they passed; but the memory was there. He told himself that if it did happen he would not scream. He would whirl and begin to shoot. He would smash the thing against a tree trunk and shatter it with flame and copper.

He was being careful to discount any tendency toward weakness and when, on a halt, he had found that each time he had pressed his back solidly against a tree he thereafter turned his back to the trail and faced the tree.

Ambu was horrified. He padded beside Lord Ginger, carrying the spare gun, wanting to offer his help, wanting to somehow comfort this huge man who was now so changed.

"Hot, eh?" said Ginger with a smile.

"Hot," said Ambu.

"Ask the trackers if we are almost there."

Ambu chattered to the men ahead and then shrugged. "They say a little way now."

"Good," said Ginger, carefully careless.

The trail began to widen and the river of sirup which ran in it began to shoal. The clearing was about them before they could see that it was and then the only sign was a certain lightness to the fog.

"Tracks!" cried the blue in advance.

Ginger went up to him. He wiped his face beneath his swamp mask and put the handkerchief carefully away. He knelt casually, taking care that his thigh boots did not ship mud and water over their tops. Impersonally he regarded the tracks.

There were six of them in sets of two. The first were clearly claws; two and a half feet behind them the second set showed no claws; two and a half feet back from these the third and last set showed claws again. The weight of the thing must be less than three hundred pounds.

A prickle of knowing went up the back of Ginger's spine. These tracks were perfect. They had been placed in a spot where they would retain their impressions. And from here they led away into the trees; but to this place they did not exist.

"Devil," chattered Ambu.

A devil was very nearly an acceptable explanation to Ginger. No six-tracked animal was known to him, either on this planet or any other.

Suddenly he stood up, no longer able to bear the feeling of attack from behind. He turned slowly. The dark vapors curled and drifted like veils through the clearing.

"Get on the track of it," said Ginger in blue.

The trackers trotted out, too swiftly for Ginger to keep up without extreme effort, but Ginger made no protest.

He told himself that the fever made him this way; but he had had fever before. Deep within he knew that the beast had a thing which belonged to Ginger, a thing which Ginger had never imagined could be stolen. And until he met that beast and killed that beast, he would not recover his own.

The tracks led on a broad way, clear in the mud, with a straight course. Uneasily, Ginger watched behind him, recalling the words of the chief that the thing often backtracked. But there were no overhanging branches in this part and that gave some relief for they had come up a gradual grade and the trail was flanked with tall, limber trees which barred no light. Here the ground was more solid even if covered with thick masses of rot and the combination of greater light and better footing caused a weight to gradually lift from Ginger's back.

And then it happened. There was a swishing, swooping sound and a scream from Ambu! Ginger spun about to scan the back trail—and to find nothing. Ambu was gone.

Ginger looked up. In a cunningly manufactured sling, not unlike a rabbit snare, held by one foot, was Ambu, thirty feet from the ground, obviously dead, his head smashed in from its contact with the trunk of the tree which, springing upright, had lifted him.

After a few moments Ginger said in a controlled voice, "Cut him down."

And some hours later the group crawled back into the compound, carrying Ambu, Ginger still walking by himself despite the greyness of his face and the strange tightness about his mouth.

With each passing day the lines on Ginger Cranston's face deepened and the hollows beneath his eyes grew darker. It was harder now to bring a proper note of cheerfulness into his commands, to reassure when all chances of success diminished with each casualty to the hunting party.

There came, one dull, drab day the final break with the blues. Ginger Cranston had seen it coming, had known that his own power had grown less and less in their eyes, that their faith in the great white hunter had slimmed to a hopeless dejection. Da juju had sapped the bulwark of morale and the battlement came sliding down like a bank of soupy Venusian mud. Ginger Cranston woke to empty tents. The great white hunter was defeated. It was inevitable that the remainder of his crew would desert and it was not necessary that the way of their going be told, for the blazing mouths of guns could not have driven them back. Seven had died. Five remained to flee and the five had fled.

"Bring me trackers," said the haggard white man.

The chief looked at the mud and regarded it with intensity. He looked at a pegunt rooting there as though he had seen such an animal for the first time. He looked at a tree with searching interest.

"I said trackers!" said Ginger Cranston.

The chief scratched himself and began to sidle away, still without meeting the eyes of the white man.

Ginger struck out and the chief crumpled

into a muddy moaning pile.

"TRACKERS!" said Ginger.

The chief turned his face into the slime and whimpered. In all the village not one blue could be observed, but one felt that all the village had seen and now dispiritedly sank into a dull apathy as though this act of brutality, borne out of temper, was not a thing to be blamed but merely a thing which proved that the great white hunter was no longer great. With all the rest, da juju had him, had his heart and soul, which was far worse than merely having his life.

Ginger turned away, ashamed and shaken. He pushed his way into his tent and mechanically wiped the rain from his face, discovering abruptly that he wept. He could not now gain back the thing which da juju had. His means were gone with his men. He could hear the chief whimpering out there in the mud, could hear a wind in the great trees all around the place, mixed with the toneless mutter of the drizzle upon the canvas.

In the metal mirror which hung on the pole, steamed though it was, Ginger caught a glimpse of his countenance. He started, for that which he saw was not in the least Ginger Cranston; it was as though even the bone structure had somehow shifted to complete another identity. He had no impulse to strike the mirror down— he was tired, achingly, horribly tired. He wanted to crawl into his bed and lie there with his face to the blank wall of canvas and never move again.

Shame was the only active emotion now,

shame for the thing he had done just now, for the chief hardly came to his shoulder and the mud-colored body was twisted by accident and illness into a caricature of a blue. Ginger took a bottle from a case and went out again into the rain.

He knelt beside the chief and sought to turn him over and make him look. But the resistless shoulder was a thing which could not be turned and the low, moaning whimper was not a thing which would stop.

"I am sorry," said Ginger.

But there was no change. Ginger set the bottle down in the mud beside the head and went back into his tent.

Slowly, soddenly, he sank upon the rubber cover of his bunk looking fixedly and unseeingly at his fouled boots. Da juju. The devil, Ambu had called him. Had not Ambu been right? For what animal could do these things and remain out of the range of a hunter's guns? Da juju—

There was a slithering, harsh sound and Ginger, blenched white, came shaking to his feet, his light gun swinging toward the movement, sweat starting from him. But there was no target. The thrown-back flap of his tent had slipped into place, moved by the wind.

He was nauseated and for seconds the feeling of claws digging into his back would not abate. He struggled with his pent sanity, sought nervously for the key of control which, more and more, was ever beyond the reach of mental fingers. The scream died unvoiced, the gun slipped to the bunk and lay there with its muzzle like a fixed, accusing eye. Hypnotically, Ginger Cranston looked at that muzzle. It threw a twenty-millimeter slug and would tear half a head from a Mamodon bull; the bullet came out when the trigger was pressed, came out with a roar of savage flame, came out with oblivion as its command. Limply Ginger regarded it. He knew very little about death, he a hunter who should have known so much. Was dead a quiet and untroubled sleep which went on forever or was death a passing to another existence? Would the wings of death carry something that was really Ginger Cranston out of this compound, away from these trees, this fog, this constant rain, this . . . this beast?

Funny he had never before considered death, odd how little he knew, he who had been so sure and proud of knowing so very much.

Death was a final conclusion—or was it a beginning? And if he took it now— Suddenly he saw where his thought led him and drew back in terror from the lip of the chasm. Then, as one wonders how far he would have fallen had he slipped, he crept cautiously back and thoughtfully regarded the bottomless, unknowable deep, finding within himself at this strange moment a power to regard such a thing with a detached attitude, to dispassionately weigh a thing which he believed it to be in his hand to choose.

He seemed to fall away from himself in body and yet stand there, an untouchable, uncaring personality who had but to extend a crooking finger and call unto himself all there was to know. Suspended in time, in action, in human thought, he regarded all he was, had been, would be. There were no words to express this identity, this timelessness, only a feeling of actually existing for the first time; layer upon layer of a nameless something had been peeled away to leave a naked, knowing thing; a mask was gone from his eyes. But when he again came to himself, still standing beside his bed, still staring at the gun, he was muddy, weary Ginger Cranston once again who could feel that something had happened but could not express even in nebulous thought any part of the occurrence. Something had changed. A decision had been born. A plan of action, a somber, solemn plan was his.

About his waist he buckled a flame pistol and into that belt he thrust a short skinning knife. He pulled up his collar and strapped his swamp mask to it. He picked up his gun and looked into its magazine.

When Ginger stepped from the tent the chief was gone but the bottle sat upright in the mud, untouched, a reproof which would have reached Ginger a few minutes before but which could not touch him now. For perhaps an hour, even a day, nothing could touch him, neither sadness nor triumph. He was still within himself, waiting for a thing he knew would come, a thing much greater than shame or sorrow. He had chosen his death for he had found it to be within his realm of choice and having chosen it he was dead. It mattered little what happened now. It mattered much that da juju would end. But it did not matter emotionally.

It was a clear concern, undiluted by self.

Walking quietly through the mud he came to the trail which led upward to the series of knolls where the trees were thinner and the ground a degree more solid. This time he was not tracking. He gave no heed to the ground for he was within the role of the hunted, not that of the hunter. He knew with a clarity not born of reason that he would be found.

Along the crest of a small hill, looking out across the foggy depths of the forest, touched faintly by the gloomy sun, he walked and knew he could be seen against the sky. He stopped a little while and dispassionately regarded the forest tops again, noting for the first time that gray was not the color there as he had always supposed, but a drab green, rust red, dark blue, and smoky yellow. It was a little thing to notice but it seemed important. He turned and walked slowly back along the crest, gun held in the crook of his arm, his body relaxed. From this end he could see the impression of the village, a vacant space in the trees, a small knoll itself, wrapped in blue-yellow cotton batting which restively shifted pattern.

About him the clouds thickened blindingly and the lenses of his swamp mask fogged. For a brief instant terror was in him before he pressed it gently down, out of sight, and buried it somewhere within him once more. The cloud lifted and curved easily away. For a little while then the sun was almost bright and it was this time upon which he had counted. He could be seen for a kilometer or more against the sky, blackly etched, motionless, waiting.

The atmosphere thickened, darkened, grew soggier with spurts of rain; the sun and any trace of it vanished even to Ginger's shadow. The time was here. He would walk slowly, leaving deep tracks, putting aside any impulse to step on stone and so break his trail. He knew *it* would follow.

He took his time, now and then pausing to arrange some imagined opening in his coat or mask, occasionally pulling off the mask altogether and lighting his pipe, to sit on a rotten log until the tobacco was wholly burned.

He had no plan of walking save that he stayed in the trees where the great branches leaned out above him like grasping hands, only half seen in the gloom.

When the dark began to settle he did not return to the village, but kept upon his circuitous way, vaguely aware that the compound was somewhere upon his right, caring very little about it.

When he could no longer see clearly he groped to the base of a great tree; he could sit here now, waiting with dull patience for the thing to happen. From his face he pulled the swamp mask. Steadying his gun against the trunk beside him he proceeded to prepare his smoke.

It happened suddenly, silently, efficiently. The vine-woven net dropped soundlessly over his head, slithered to his feet and then with swift ferocity, yanked tight and brought him with a crash into the mud!

There was a scurrying about him as though something leaped up and down, darted back and forth to swiftly study the situation so as to re-quire a minimum of effort in the final kill.

Ginger's right hand sought to grip the flame pistol at his thigh, but he could not bend his arm; his left hand clawed insensately at the net and a scream of terror welled up in his throat. He stilled the beating of the hand. He pressed back the scream. He reached to his belt and drew the knife with a deliberate swiftness and an economy of effort. The keen edge bit into the tough fibers of the vine, cleared it away from half his side, began to slice it off his ankles. And then the thing struck!

The foul animal smell of it assailed him, more acute that the bite of the claws which went through his jacket and into his side like a set of bayonets.

He sensed the downward drive of the other claws and caught a blurred glimpse of the thing. The slimy fur of the leg was in his fingers and the striking paw missed his face.

Ginger jabbed upward with the knife and felt it saw vainly into the thing. With a scream the beast twisted away and with it went the knife.

There was a brief interval before the next, more savage attack, and in that space Ginger cleared his feet of the net. When it struck him again, like a battering ram with force enough to smash in his ribs, he was able to come up to his knees and fumble for his flame pistol while fending with his left arm. He had no more than drawn the gun when a scrambling kick set it flying into the mud, far from reach.

A cold piece of metal banged Ginger in the

mouth and he snatched hungrily for the haft of his flesh-imbedded knife. Slippery as his fingers were, he retained it, drew it forth. He kicked out with his feet and then drove the keen steel deep into the body of the thing!

With a shudder it fell back, a claw weakly seeking to strike again and then falling away. There was a threshing, rattling sound and Ginger drew away, trying to clear his sight, fumbling with the other hand for his gun which he knew had been at the base of the tree. He had the weapon in his hand before he could see. There was water in a footprint which his hand had touched and he quickly bathed his eyes.

The light was faint, too faint to show more than a dark blob stretched in the muck, a blob which didn't move now. Ginger warily skirted it, keeping it covered, fumbling for a flash inside his waterproof coat.

The cold, impersonal beam played upon the object, raked it from end to end and then strayed uncertainly back to the head.

Ginger knelt and unfastened the straps of the frayed, worn leatherlike suit that clothed the corpse and laboriously turned it over. Metal-tipped space gloves clicked as the arms flopped against each other. There was an almost illegible trace of lettering on the back, fouled with mud and blood, torn in spots. "SP—E SHIL—" it said, before a gouge tore out the ship's name. Below, "Spacepo—Lowry, U-A."

It stank with dried and rotted blood and meat of long-gone kills, and the unwashed body of its occupant.

Ginger turned it back and looked again at the face. Identification was hopeless. The disastrous landing had gouged and torn the face half away; there was a deep dent in the forehead where the skull had been broken inward, and an angry, seamed and cross-seamed welt told of slow healing without the slightest rudiment of attention.

Ginger straightened slowly, gathered his things from the ground, and squelched off on his back-trail. Native bearers would have to carry that beast home. The beast some unknown and probably unknowable crash of a small tramp spacer had made from a man. A ruthless, pure animal—with all the cunning of human intelligence still left in the damaged brain.

Ginger swung along the trail in the long, easy strides of a huntsman of standing. There were bruises, and certain scratches that twinged a bit, but that sort of damage was of no importance. The great thing was—a thing Ginger now scarcely realized—that he had recaptured that quite intangible reality that had been stolen from him.

The Invaders

THE LANDING PRISON SHIP HOVERED A SPACE above the field as though arrested by the titanic battle in progress below, but in reality only waiting for the assembly of a securing crew.

The Crystal Mines, beyond the mystery of the Black Nebula and in a world unlike anything anywhere in space outside, rippled in the waves of heat and shuddered under the rapid impact of fast-firing arc cannon. A desolate and grim outpost, the last despair of convicts for seventy-five years, the latest hope of a fuel-starved empire of space, racked continually by attack.

The Crystal Mines, where disgraced officers came to battle through their last days against forces which had as yet defied both analysis and weapon. Heartbreak and misery and war beneath a roof of steel and upon strangely quivering ground, amid vapors and gasses which put commas and then periods to the lives of the luckless criminals sent here as a punishment transcending in violence even slow execution.

Gedso Ion Brown stood at the port in awed silence, caught by the unleashed fury in the scene below and forgetting even the danger and mystery of their course into this place. For here below had come to being things more strange than any described in the folklore of any planet in a setting which he realized no man could adequately describe.

Below were metal blocks, the mine barracks and offices, sufficient to house half a million men. They crept up the side of a concave cliff like a stairway until they nearly touched the embedded edge of the mine roof. Curving down into the white stones of the valley was a spun silica wall a hundred meters high, studded at thirty-pace intervals by cannon turrets. The mine, the roof, the wall, all were contained in an immense cavern which was reached through a hundred-and-eighty kilometer tunnel seven kilometers in diameter. This huge inner chamber was perhaps seventy-five kilometers wide and two hundred long and had its own ceiling fourteen kilometers above the uneven floor.

The light had no apparent source, seeming to exude from cliffs and ceiling and ground, possibly from the perfectly formed, sharp boulders, the size of ships, strewn everywhere, lodged everywhere, even hanging from the ceiling. These were a translucent white and constituted the product of the mine.

Up and down the wall went the lashing trajectories of the arc cannon, raking over the scorched and smoking ground, reaching in hysterical fury at the lumbering attackers.

Gedso Ion Brown put a pocket glass to his eye and looked wonderingly at the scene. He had heard here and there through space that such things had existed. He had reserved judgment for one could never tell what tale might next crawl through the vast spaces of the Empire. But the descriptions he had heard, probably because no man ever came back from the Crystal Mines unless he was a high officer, had been gross underestimates.

Gedso Ion Brown closed his pocket glass and put it into his shabby tunic. He was not of delicate constitution and he had been near too many battles to become shaky about anything. Further, nervousness was not part of his temperament. But he did not want to look at those things.

The spaceship was settling down to the charred landing field with its miserable cargo and Gedso Ion Brown turned back to his pinched cabin, one of the only two which had no leg irons included, to pack his slender belongings. A little later he shuffled down a gangway and put his trunk on the ground and looked about for someone to tell him where his quarters were. But there was no one interested in him and so he stood with his baggy uniform blowing about his ungainly body, feeling unwelcome and forlorn.

A mass gangway to his right, like a leg of a rusty beetle, was crowded with the sullen freight brought here each trip. Convicts, emaciated and ragged and chafed by irons, were being herded into trucks by surly and ruthless guards. A regiment of criminal soldiers, branded by their black collars and lack of hand weapons, were forming under the ships' belly.

Gedso wondered if the commandant knew of his coming and looked nearsightedly toward the faraway P.C. where floated the tricolored banner of the Empire. Guards and hard-stamped officers passed him by without speaking. Gedso felt even more alone and unwelcome.

He was not a prepossessing figure, Gedso Ion Brown. He was a full two meters tall and he weighed two and one-half times as much as another the same size for he had been born on Centaur One of Vega to pioneer Earth parents and Vega's Centaur One has a gravity two and one-half times that of Earth. A shuffling gait, a forward cant to his disproportionate head and thick, round shoulders minimized his appearance.

Life to him had always been a travail. At his Earth engineering school he had been dubbed a "Provincial lout" and he had earned it for he crushed whatever chair he sat upon and in an unthinking moment might pull a door off its hinges if the catch held a second too long—and then stand looking stupidly and embarrassedly at the thing he held by the knob. Awkward and ungainly and shy, Gedso Ion Brown had never made much way in the Extra-Territorial Scienticorps, getting his promotion by number and so progressing alone and ignored in a service vast enough to swallow even his unhandsome bulk.

People generally thought him stupid, basing their conclusions upon his social disgraces, but this was not fair. In his line Gedso was alert enough and it is doubtful if more than two or three men knew of that trick of his of glancing at a page and mentally photographing the whole of it. In such a way Gedso studied. In such a way did he hide his only shining light. He had two vices—apples and puzzles—and the only baggage he had placed in the freight room contained nothing else.

The arc cannon crackled with renewed ferocity and he looked away from the things he could see lumbering beyond the far wall. Convinced at last that his arrival was going unremarked, he tucked the heavy trunk under his arm and shuffled toward the P.C. Jostled by guards hurrying in and out of the place, he put down his burden and sat on it.

A trusty orderly jabbed his back with a juice wand. "You're blocking the way."

Gedso looked at the narrow, evil face and shifted his trunk farther off the walk and sat down again with an embarrassed apology.

"What do you want?" said the trusty. "You can't hang around here all day."

"I'd like to see the commanding officer," said Gedso.

"He's busy."

"I'll wait," said Gedso uncomfortably. He took an apple out of his pocket and shined it on his tunic sleeve.

The breeze which blew up from the wall two kilometers away was acrid with brimstone and hot with the stench of death. Officers and runners came and went, a two-way stream of weary, sick men. Gedso noticed, after a while, that they were all of one expression on leaving the squat building no matter their expressions when they arrived. When they came out they looked scared and whipped, and Gedso began to form an idea of the character of the commander within.

"You still around here?" said the orderly. "You can't throw garbage in this yard!"

Gedso picked up the apple core he had dropped and put its dusty brownness in his pocket. Time slogged slowly onward. The crackling along the wall eased and the shapes were no longer visible beyond. Gedso tugged at the orderly's sleeve, carefully lest he break the man's arm.

"Would you please tell the commander that I would like to see him?"

"What's your name? What do you want to see him about?"

"My name is Brown. Gedso Ion Brown. I'm a technician in the E-T.S. I've been ordered here."

The orderly looked startled and then weak. He nearly dropped his juice wand as he whipped to attention. "I . . . I am s-s-s-sorry, sir. The c-c-commander will be informed immediately, s-s-s-sir." He dived into the post and came skidding back to attention. "The commander will see you immediately, sir. I . . . I did not have any idea you were a technician, sir. I did not see your insignia, sir."

Gedso said mildly, "Will you watch my trunk?" and went on inside.

154

The secretary, a convict soldier with the chevrons of master sergeant on his blouse, opened the door into an inner room. Gedso ambled through.

Jules Drummond, captain general of the Administrative Department's Extra-Territorial Command Corps, looked sourly up from the manifests of the newly arrived space vessel. He was a thin, dark gentleman, very tall and very military. His face had never known a smile and his eyes nothing but disdain. He was half ill with the vapors of this gigantic pest hole and, at intervals, mechanically dosed himself from a rack of bottles in the arm of his chair. There was a look of hawk cruelty about him, a look so common to E-T. C.C. commanders and intensified in General Drummond.

He looked for a full minute at Gedso and then said, "So you are a technician, are you?" With intentional rudeness he looked back at the manifest and left Gedso standing there. After a while he snapped, "Sit down."

Gedso squirmed in discomfort and looked at the frail chairs. He pretended to ease into one, but held himself up from it.

"Where are your orders?" said Drummond.

Gedso fumbled through the baggy pockets of his tunic, found three apples and a core, but, much to his embarrassment, no orders. Faltering he said, "I guess—I must have packed them."

"Humph!" said Drummond. "The next time you report to me at least wear insignia."

"I'll get the orders," said Gedso. He went out and got them from his trunk.

Drummond again ordered him to sit down. It did not occur to Gedso to resent such treatment. He was only nominally under orders from General Drummond, for the Scienticorps was too important and too powerful to be ordered about by E-T.C.C. officers.

Acidly, Dummond threw the orders on the desk before him. "Two months ago I phoned for a technician. The fools! They know what the catalyzer from these mines is worth. They know how important it is that we work unhampered. And if they don't know that we expend more men in fighting than we do in mining, they are stupid! Political fools, bungling the affairs of the Empire! They send me prisoners on their last leg with disease instead of workmen and artisans! They send me drunkards and worse for officers. By the look of it they want us to be driven from here, want the mines to close! I beg for a technician. A real technician to do something about this continual warfare. I tell them that day by day it grows worse and that it is only a question of time before all of us will be devoured alive!"

"I am a technician, sir," ventured Gedso timidly. "I'd like to do what I can to help."

Drummond seared him with a glare which took in the soiled and wrinkled slacks, the oversize tunic with its too-short sleeves, the eyes peering nearsightedly from behind thick spectacles and the unkempt mass of tow hair which further impeded vision.

"The final decadence of Empire," said Drummond nastily.

Gedso seemed to miss the insult. "If you could get somebody to tell me what is wrong—"

"What would *you* do about it?" said Drummond. "I'll send an engineer. Now get out of here!"

Gedso slipped as he rose from the chair and sat back with his full weight. It splintered to atoms under him and the whole post shook. Scarlet and confused, Gedso backed up through the door.

From the office soared Drummond's voice as the general looked tragically up toward an unheeding deity. "The Crystal Mines, the most vital and important post in all space, the most valuable command any man can be given! And they send me fools, fools, fools!" He threw himself dramatically upon his desk with a despairing sob.

The orderly was a mental chameleon. When he dropped Gedso out of the passenger truck before the isolated little hut reserved for Extra-Territorial Scienticorps men in case they might come to inspect, the orderly did not offer to help Gedso with his trunk or even go so far as to hope that Gedso was comfortable. The orderly who, after the fashion of orderlies, had had an ear glued to the wall of Drummond's office, hurried away to spread, after the fashion of orderlies, his commander's opinion of the latest addition to the staff of the Crystal Mines.

That this was true was indicated by the attitude of the third-rank combat engineer who slouched up to the hut two hours later and found Gedso lying on the hard bunk.

All his life, Blufore, the third-rank engineer, had heard tales of the technicians of the E-T. S., but only twice before today had he seen a technician first class in the flesh and not until today had he spoken to one of the "miracle men." Glorified in song and story, in spacecast and rumor, E-T. S. technicians, "trouble shooters of our far-flung lifelines," "magicians in khaki," "test-tube godlings," seemed to have a right to awe. There were twenty-seven thousand of them spread out amid a hundred and eighty-five trillion beings, things and men who held down the habitable spots of space, and a technician first class was, reputedly, never sent to duty unless everything was gone awry. Blufore had come ready to discard the flying rumors and bad opinions of this technician, for he knew that the technician's presence was the Grand Council's most scathing criticism of a military administrator.

Blufore saw the ungainly hulk of Gedso Ion Brown sprawled upon the bed. Blufore saw no test tubes or servant monsters. And when Blufore heard the mild, almost stuttering voice bid him, "Come in," Blufore reacted as would any man experiencing the downfall of a god. He was ready to kick the chunks around.

Gedso looked nearsightedly at Blufore as the man sat down. Gedso did not like the swaggering, boasting expression on Blufore's face or the precision of Blufore's fancifully cut uniform. Blufore made him most uneasy.

"I came to give you the data on this mess," said Blufore. "But there's nothing anybody can do which hasn't already been done. I know because I've been here for eighteen months. I know because as a combat engineer I've tried every form of repelling force known without result on the 'things.' Now what do you want to know?"

Gedso was not offended. He swung down his feet and cupped his chin and looked at Blufore. "Just what are these 'things'?"

"Monsters, maybe. Living tanks. Some of them weigh a hundred and fifty tons, some three hundred. Some have a front that is all bone mouth. Some have eighty to a hundred and twenty legs. Some are transparent. Some are armor-plated. There have been as many as five thousand dead before the wall, making a wall of their own, and the others have kept right on coming. I suppose half a million of them have been killed by arc cannon in the past five or six years. Sometimes the push is so bad from the back that the dead are shoved like a shield right up to and through the wall and the things behind start grabbing soldiers. We lose about two hundred men a week."

"How long has this present battle lasted?" said Gedso.

"Seventy-five years. Since the day the Terrestrial Exploration Command moved in here and found the crystals. First we fought them with ranked space tanks. Then with a force field. Then with fire guns. And now with arc cannon. They can be killed, yes. But that never stops them. Their attacks are in greater or lesser ferocity, but are spaced evenly over a period of time. Intense for an Earth week.

159

Slack for an Earth week. Intense for an Earth week. Over and over. This is a slack period. They have broken through the wall just once, yesterday. They've been at this attack for seventy-five years."

"You don't know what they are, then?"

"Nobody knows and nobody ever will," said Blufore.

"Have to ask," apologized Gedso. "Ask a question, get an answer. Have to ask. Is there anything else peculiar about this place?"

"Peculiar! You must have seen it from the outside. You come through a wall of ink a thousand light-years long and high and three light-years thick. And inside the Black Nebula there are no stars or space as we know it, but gigantic shapes, dark and vague. And the space has force in it which heats a ship scorching hot and knocks it around like a cork in a dynamo. And you come in here through a tunnel to get to a chamber whch is light but has no sun, where the most valuable catalyst ever found lies all over and even sticks from the ceiling. Peculiar! The mystery of this continued, seventy-five-year attack is nothing compared to the bigger mystery."

Gedso said, "Are there any other tunnels leading out from this chamber?"

"I suppose there may be. It is too dangerous to scout. And there is no need to go beyond."

"I see," said Gedso.

"And within another month we will probably have to abandon this place," said Blufore, in a lower tone. "The wall out there was high enough once. Now it isn't. The arc cannons have less and less effect upon the 'things.' Each weapon has at first been adequate and then has become useless. And now there is no weapon to replace the arc cannon. We'll have to abandon the Crystal Mines and the Empire can go to hell for its catalysts. And, between us, I can't say as I particularly care."

"I see," said Gedso, blinking his eyes like a sleepy pelican grown elephant size.

"You can't do anything about it," said Blufore.

"Maybe not," said Gedso.

"That's all I can tell you," said Blufore.

"Thank you," said Gedso.

Blufore left without the courtesy of awaiting a dismissal.

Gedso put a couple of apples in his pocket and shuffled out into the gaseous light. He stood for a little while listening to the arc cannon crackle and blast and then moved slowly toward the wall, stepping off the road when cars and line trucks dashed by.

He climbed a stairway up to an observation post and hesitated near the top when he saw an army lieutenant and a signalman there.

"No visitors allowed," snapped the lieutenant.

"Excuse me," said Gedso and backed down.

He went to the outer wall and climbed to a command post there which he made certain was empty. He wiped his glasses and gazed through the dome out across the broken plain.

Somehow he could not get the "things" in focus at all and, for him, they moved as gigantic blurs, agleam with the savage light of exploding electricty from the arc cannon. The horde reached far, a moving, seemingly insensate sea, pushing forward into the glare of battle.

A convict private scuttled into the dome from the turret, beating out the flame which charred his tunic. He saw Gedso and started, but then saw no insignia and relaxed.

"Damn fuses. Six billion kilo-volts," volunteered the private, gazing ruefully at his burned hands. He was a snub-nosed little fellow, slight of build, hard-boiled in a go-to-hell sort of way. He fixed a curious eye on Gedso. "What are you doin' around here? You ain't a tourist, are you?"

"Well—" hesitated Gedso.

"Heard a party of tourists came here once. Thought it'd be fun. Two died of shock and the rest took the same ship back. Friend of somebody?"

"No," said Gedso. "I guess not. You must have been around this place for a long while."

"Four solar years and a butt," he pointed with a grin at his black collar. "Stripe soldier ever since I put ten passengers and an officer into Uranus on the Jupiter shuttle. They got wings. I got a dog collar. I gotta be gettin' back to the gun before some sergeant spots me and hands out some black-and-blue drill. There's worse things than fightin' them 'things.' You got a gun when you're up here."

"Don't you ever get—upset up here?"

"Upset? Hell, pal, I had to either get over that or go nutty. I'm so varnished with inhuman feelings that I take one look at them 'things' and give 'em the works." But there was sudden change of expression in his eyes which belied his bold words. "I gotta get back to that gun."

"Have you any ideas on how to stop them?" said Gedso.

"Me? Hell, if I had any ideas it would be on the subject of desertion or mayhem to non-coms. Look at them 'things,' would you? By the bats of Belerion, I killed a hundred today if I killed one and there they are gone and live ones in their places."

"You mean they eat their own dead?"

"Naw. The dead ones sink into the ground in two or three hours and disappear. Look, I'll blast a couple."

The private went back into his turret and Gedso ambled along at his heels. Gedso made the small room somewhat crowded, but the private could have jumped through knotholes and so was not much inconvenienced.

The arc cannon's twin electrodes thrust outward, weighty because of the repelling magnet between which kicked the center of the arc half a kilometer in a broadening egg-shaped line. Stewie, or so read the letters on his back below the number, fitted a big fuse into the clips and sat down on the cannon ledge, hands grasping levers. His bright, brown eyes peered through the reducing glass which served as a sight and Gedso, behind him, found that he also could see through it.

The attack was developing out front as the things lumbered forward, breasting a force field and treading shakingly upon the flaming ground. Turrets to the right and left were blasting away. Stewie put his weapon into operation by the flip of a switch.

An arc made a loop about a meter in diameter and then, as it heated up, began to leap outward like a stretched band. The noise grew and grew and the brilliance of the arc, though cut by the glare shield, became hurtful to the eyes.

The "things" had pushed in a salient before this turret, but now into either side of that one in advance the arc began to play. Seen in the reduction glass, its outlines were almost clear. A great blob. No legs. A mouth with horizontal bone lining which now ground together, opened and shut. The thing came on, flanked on either side by a different sort.

Gedso blinked when he saw that the arc, gauged around six billion kilo-volts and five thousand amperes, had no perceptible effect upon the gigantic target. As the things came on there were fourteen of them linked abreast by the arc. Force field. Flaming earth white tongued with heat. Six billion—

Gedso looked at Stewie and saw how white the little fellow was getting around the mouth. He was affected by more than what field came through the insulator panel which protected him from it.

"Stop," snarled Stewie. "Stop, you waddling blankety blank blanks! Take it you hell-gulping blobs of stink. *Stop!*"

On came the salient. With the casual precision of well-trained troops, things to the right and left fought forward to keep the flanks of the bulge covered. Arcs from turrets all up and down the line gave the sight a jumpy, yellow glare. Behind the salient an illimitable mass was gathering, ready to rush through any break.

There was no sound but the crackle of arcs and the hiss of the white-heated ground. Pushing over crystalline boulders the size of houses as a man might roll a pebble underfoot, the legions pressed forward.

Sweat was dripping from Stewie. His thumb was easing the range expertly. His trained body reacted in unison with the targets' every shift.

A quarter of a kilometer. Half of that. A hundred meters. Fifty meters. Ten meters. In the reduction sight the heads of the foremost filled the field. Eyeless, expressionless. Gaping caverns of mouths.

Stewie was almost depressed to the limit of the weapon. He was swearing in high-pitched gibberish at the wall men in his immediate vicinity, though they could not, of course, hear him.

The bulge was against the wall. The wall trembled. Fulminating acid was suddenly dumped from huge caldrons on either side of each turret. The torrents splashed devastatingly upon the ranks.

The wall began to shake and then teeter backward.

A scale filled the whole field of the reduction sight. With a crunch the top of the turret sagged, showering Gedso and the gunner with shivered splinters of transparent, shell-proof, heat-proof, failure-proof battleglass.

Stewie's ledge swept down and the electrodes of the cannon swooped up with savage fury. A huge spot on a scale was visible, taking the full impact of the concentrated fire.

Gedso let drive with a blasting wand. This and the arc had the sudden effect of lashing the scale spot into flame. It moved on. The flame spread out. It became roasting hot in the turret and Stewie ducked under a floorplate, tugging anxiously at Gedso's shoelace to get him down. The floorplate clanked into space and Gedso flipped on a fingernail torch. Stewie was trying to grin, but he was racked by shudders. There were flecks of lather in the corners of his mouth and a not-quite-sane light in his eyes.

The wall began to sway anew and then, with earthquake abruptness, shook like the dice in a cup about the dog cell. Gedso put a hand out and pinned Stewie to the far wall to ease the strain of the shock. There was a final crash and then quiet descended save for the far-off *snap-snap-snap* of mobile guns.

"They're *through*," said Stewie, steadying his voice with an effort. "They're between us and the barracks; they're being fought by tanks and pillboxes." A shudder took hold of him and he fought it off. "That's what's been happening more and more often for two months. They care less and less about arc cannon. First time, four years ago, arc cannon stopped 'em like mowing down weenies at a picnic. Now we'll get a new weapon, maybe, and it will last a couple of years. All we do is toughen them up! One weapon. The next. And what the hell's the use of it? They tell me there's nothing that can do more damage than a cannon like you saw up there."

There was a lurch and then another and Stewie whispered, dead-eyed, "The 'things' heard us and they're looking for us. *Ssshh!*"

They sat in silence, shaken now and then, hearing stones and spun silica crush under weight.

Gedso took out the two apples and gave one to Stewie who repressed a nervous giggle and bit avidly into it. The gesture had not been intended as a demonstration of aplomb, but Stewie took it that way and appreciated it.

Ninety-three minutes later, by Gedso's watch, all movement in the rubbish ceased. The *snap-snap-snap* dwindled away.

There was silence.

"Either there isn't any mine," said Stewie, "or our birds got rid of them."

They waited a little time in order to be sure that the "things" no longer snuffled about the wreck of the wall and then Gedso went to work. Stewie was stricken with awed respect at the sight of the seemingly commonplace Gedso pushing out of the rubble like a super-drive tank, so much amazed, in fact, that he nearly forgot to follow. When Gedso was on top of the blasted remains he made sure all was clear and then, reaching down, snagged Stewie's collar and yanked him forth like a caught minnow.

The break had not been without damage to the inner defenses for two towers spread their disassembled parts upon the ground and a rampart was crushed like a slapped cardboard box. A thousand-yard section of the outer wall had been smashed and lay like an atomized dust pile.

A clearing crew, hauling a dead "thing" behind four huge tractors, stopped work to stare in surprise at the pair who had erupted from the debris.

Gedso and Stewie picked their way over the scored and littered ground, depressed by the fumes arising from the mountainous dead "things." A silica spinning sled almost knocked them down as it rushed to the repair of the defenses and as they leaped out of the way an officer spotted the convict uniform. Stewie was snatched up and cast into the arms of a straggler patrol which flashed away without any attention to Gedso's protest.

That evening—or at the beginning of the third period—Gedso sat at the table in his quarters eating his dinner out of a thermocan and gazing thoughtfully at the murky shadows in the far corner of the room. He was intent upon his problem to such an extent that he only occasionally remembered to take a bite.

New weapons. Year in and year gone combat engineers had invented new means of knocking down the menacing legions. And certainly, with the power available, there seemed no more lethal weapon than the arc cannon—for here it was evolved to a point over the horizon from weapons used in the remainder of space.

The invention of another weapon, even if that could be accomplished would not prove wholly efficacious for it would only last two or three years and then yet another would have to be compounded.

His door was thrust inward and General Drummond stood there looking at him. Drummond's eyes were bloodshot and his mouth twitched at the right corner.

Gedso was confused by the unusualness of the visit and hastened to leap up—spilling the thermocan's gravy across the bare board.

Drummond flung himself into a chair. "I'm worn out. Worn out! The responsibility, the greatness of the command, the rotten character of aid—" He looked fixedly at Gedso. "When will your new weapon be ready?"

"I . . . I don't think I am going to build one," faltered Gedso. "There is nothing better than an arc cannon."

Drummond sagged. "Served by fools. Strangled in red tape. The most valuable command in the Empire left with no attention to its need. I'm hardly used. Hardly." He straightened up and looked at Gedso, addressing him directly. "You were sent here to invent a new weapon," said Drummond harshly. "You are going to invent it. I know that I cannot command an E-T.S. officer unless in a situation where my command itself is threatened with extinction. The command is threatened. I, General Drummond, have the power to demand of you a means of stopping the attackers. If I do not receive one in a very few days, I shall be forced to accomplish your recall. I have influence enough to do that."

"My orders," said Gedso, "read that I must

investigate the threat to the area here and achieve a means of lessening or removing that threat if it exists." He recoiled from contradicting Drummond, a general, for any human contact made his shyness acute. But he knew he was well within his own rights. "I do not think a new weapon can be evolved and I do not think its effectiveness would be final, no matter how good it might be. I must ask for means to inspect this entire area—"

"Blufore intimated," said Drummond, "that you did not intend to set to work immediately. That is why I came here. I also happen to know regulations. If I wish to effect your recall and replacement, I must give you notice of it in writing. Your interference today on the outer defenses caused a breach to be made in them. I have the full report from an officer and gunners in flanking turrets who saw you go there and saw the fire cease in the turret you approached. You interfered with a gunner on duty. Here are the signed affidavits. I did not intend to submit them if you had actually worked out a means of improving our defenses. My procedure is correct and not to be questioned. Here are your copies of my demand for a new technician. The originals will be facsimile transmitted within the hour."

Drummond rose and looked at Gedso. "You see, my powers are not small and my command far too important to be slighted by anyone, much less yourself." He threw the papers on the table, where the gravy immediately stained them, and started out.

"Wait," said Gedso, "tell me what happened

to the gunner!"

"That is a military matter and is in no way within your province." Drummond again would have left, but an arm shot across the doorway —Gedso had moved with such swiftness that Drummond could not believe the heavy fellow had crossed the room.

"You mean you are going to punish him?"

Drummond replied, "It is to be regretted that we cannot punish all those who affect our operations in so summary a manner."

"You are going to execute him?"

"That is the penalty."

Gedso faltered, but only for a moment. "If . . . if you will drop that sentence, I will guarantee to bring peace to these mines in five days."

Drummond knew he had a winning card. "I can suspend the sentence until you do, if we must bargain for what is actually a duty. That is a very wild offer," he added, "in the light that peace has not been brought to this place in seventy-five years of constant endeavor by the greatest engineers of the Empire."

"Release him to me and I will do it in four days!"

"Wilder still. But—it is a bargain. If you fail, of course, the sentence goes back into effect. That, naturally, is understood. And now, if you will be so good as to step aside, I will relieve myself of your company."

Drummond left and Gedso wandered back to the table to stand there fingering the copies without being wholly aware of them. The folly of his statement was beginning to grow upon him, and he could not clearly understand what strange emotional forces had so led him to stake his reputation. And then he remembered half-pint Stewie with the snub nose and the grin and sighed with relief. There was just a chance— Gedso dropped upon his knees beside his baggage and began to haul forth engineering treatises.

The scout ship vibrated nervously as her tubes warmed as though she shivered at the consideration of the cruise she was about to undertake or, again, in annoyance with the agitation and harshness in the voices of the group of men who stood at her side on the ground.

"It was my belief that you only intended an aerial examination of the mines," said Blufore haughtily.

Gedso's tone was patient. "The character of this area has never truly been determined. It will be necessary to go outside and perhaps even to the Black Nebula itself. Unless I am allowed to make the examination I cannot collect facts with which to work."

"I fail to see," said Blufore, "what an examination of 'outside' has to do with fashioning a weapon to stop these attacks. My orders are specific. I am to act for General Drummond and supervise the interests of his command. It is very unusual to let anyone have a scout and it is unheard of to penetrate 'outside' with such a ship!"

"And yet," sighed Gedso, "I must go out there."

"You have already wasted a day," said Blufore. "And now you waste another and perhaps a scout as well."

The pilot, a dark-visaged officer who seemed to be made of *roccill* from the way he smelled, reeled a trifle and said, "That finishes it. I can determine when and where I will take my ship and I'm not taking her 'outside' and I don't care if the E-T.S. complains until the end of space!" So saying, he marched off.

"And I," said Blufore, "do not consider it wise to expose a piece of government property to such danger and so refuse to accompany you, thus preventing our departure, for the orders are specific in that I am to accompany you."

"I am sorry you are afraid," said Gedso.

"Fear?" said Blufore, stung. "I have no knowledge of the meaning of fear, sir. But discretion in the expenditure of government property is the first function of a combat engineer—"

"Then you have to go with us or we cannot go?" said Gedso.

"Just so," said Blufore haughtily.

A much overburdened little man came up and began to dump bits of equipment through the hatch. Stewie looked pale after his ordeal with the penalty bureau, but his eye was bright. Stewie had been bowed with awe at the intelligence that his companion in the battle had been a Scienticorps technician, but awe, with Stewie, was not of long duration.

"What happened to the pilot?" said Stewie from the top of the ship.

"He refused to go," said Gedso.

"And what is wrong with this guy?" said Stewie, pointing with a disrespectful finger.

"If he doesn't go with us, our permission is canceled," replied Gedso.

Stewie went on dumping equipment in the hatch while Blufore, ignoring a convict gunner as a self-respecting combat engineer should, went on with the finale of obstructing Gedso. There is a certain glory in being able to talk strongly and disrespectfully to one to whom one should salute with reverence.

Abruptly, Blufore's clear and melodious voice ceased and Blufore dropped heavily to the ground. The thermocan which Stewie had dropped on his head rolled a little way and then stopped.

Stewie glanced around to see if anyone had noticed and then said urgently to Gedso, "Hand him up. The orders don't say nothing about what *condition* he has to be in to go, do they?"

Gedso hesitated for a moment. "But the pilot—"

"Even if I ain't touched one of these for years and years, I can still make 'em do tricks," said Stewie. "Hand him up!"

Gedso handed up Blufore and they dropped him into the hatch.

A few seconds later the scout ship was aloft.

When Blufore at last came around, several hours later, he received the vague impression that he was being shaken by demons and kicked by *Faj* men. But such was not the case. The scout cruiser was being battered about by a hurricane of bright-yellow wind and running from darkness into light with such rapidity that the change constituted an aching vibration.

Blufore, seeing a convict jacket on the man at the controls, thought himself the victim of an attempt at escape, particularly since he himself was strongly strapped into an observer's seat. Then he caught sight of the technician.

Braced by four lashed lines which ended in eyebolts, Gedso was standing before the port, busy with a big shiny box from which came a loud and continual sequence of clicks. Beyond Gedso, Blufore could see the towering vagueness of the "outside" and the aspect of this, combined with the space sickness caused by the violent and unsteady motion of the tiny craft, made Blufore very sorry for himself.

"Go back!" he whimpered. "Go back before we are torn apart!"

Stewie said, "Shall I hit him?"

Gedso was too intent on his work to answer.

Blufore subsided and resigned himself to an agonizing doom. He knew so well that two out of every three space freighters sent back from the Crystal Mines never arrived at all, were never heard from again, and it was thought that they vanished while traversing the Black Nebula. His only hope was that they would return to the mines in a short while. And then the ports went dark and stayed dark. They were within the Black Nebula. Blufore fainted, both from illness and terror.

He had no means of knowing how long they were inside the darkness for they were in the light when he came around. They could not have gone through for that would have taken many, many hours. Perhaps now they were going back to the mines. Perhaps even yet they might return alive from this. Then horror struck him down again. They swooped into a turn and the dread black mists shut off the light anew.

From a long way off Blufore heard the series of clicks and opened his eyes to the yellow hurricane once more.

"Want to go through again?" said Stewie to Gedso.

"One more time. I think we might possibly get some results if we keep it up long enough."

"You're the boss," said Stewie, swinging the cruiser back into the darkness.

Running the rim, stabbing into and out of the Black Nebula! Like a couple of schoolboys amusing themselves playing with a high-tension wire. Blufore bethought himself of all those vanished ships and, with a groan, collapsed.

Gedso was giving Blufore a drink of something acrid when that officer next knew anything. But Blufore was too spacesick to swallow. He looked with tortured mien upon the fiend he had begun to conceive in Gedso. It was dark outside, and the cabin lights gave the technician a terrifying bulk.

"Are we—still inside it?" gulped Blufore.

"No. We are trying to find the entrance to the mines and it is somewhat difficult to do in the darkness."

Blufore tried to peer through the black port, but could see nothing. Yet Stewie was flying at full speed and without a sign of caution.

"You'll be all right soon," said Gedso sympathetically.

Blufore moaned, "I'll never be—all right again. Never."

"I'll say you won't," growled Stewie, a shadowy gnome against the lighted panel. "If you yap-yap when we get home."

But a man of Blufore's disposition could never miss the opportunity of getting another in trouble.

Hours later, in his quarters, Gedso hunched over a Black Nebula pilot, entrenched by stacks of transmographs and log tables, eating abstractedly upon an apple. Stewie sat in the corner on his black, convict blankets, his eyes closed and his head thrown back, worn out, but not admitting anything of the kind. He would partially wake each time Gedso muttered into his study and then, hearing phrases meaningless to him, would relapse into his semi-slumber. Finally Stewie fell out full length and began to snore gently. When he awoke again he was completely refreshed—and Gedso, even more deeply entrenched in scratch paper and reference books and apple cores, was still working.

Stewie got up with the intention of finding some breakfast, a search in which he was most eager, for good food was not listed among the doubtful benefits of convict soldiers.

"Make mine milk," said Gedso and went right on working.

When Stewie had finished his repast, Gedso

stood up and began to thrust notes into his pockets.

"You got an idea?" said Stewie.

"Perhaps," said Gedso. "But if we can get permission to go where we have to go, the recent excursion will be mild by comparison. Are you sure you wish to accompany me?"

"Don't gimme that," said Stewie, and he tagged the towering Gedso out across the parade ground.

Drummond was at his desk, drinking thick green *britt* and waiting for a target upon which he could vent his frustrations.

"No!" said Drummond. "I have already heard in full how you went about your last trip. This is all complete nonsense! You seem to have no realization that this is the most important command of the Empire and that its affairs must be handled in the most exemplary manner possible! You have abused one of my very best combat engineers and you have over-reached the authority you were given."

"I accumulated certain data," said Gedso hesitantly. "Perhaps I may be able to do something if I am allowed to have a company of troops."

"You know as well as I that technicians have no power to command troops."

"But I want a company of engineers," said Gedso. "If they have to fight very much, it will be my fault."

"If they are to construct a weapon of your planning, you may have them, but you cannot set foot outside the mines!"

"This area," said Gedso, "has never been examined properly. We have gone outside and now we must go deeper into the tunnels."

"Nonsense. You would be engulfed by the 'things' before you had reached a point thirty kilometers hence. This is folly and stupidity! We must have a weapon and you were given five days in which to make it. You have not so much as started and you have only two days left! I am no ordinary officer, Technician Brown. No ordinary officer would be given such an important command as this. I have influence and by the Seven Moons of Sirius' Bethel, I'll show you that you cannot snap your fingers in my face, defy my advice, exceed my instructions and then refuse to do as I dictate for the good of my command. The complaint has been transmitted and I intend to follow it with all vigor. Devise that weapon and I will do what I can to mitigate the severity of the reprimand you will certainly receive."

"Then you refuse to give me any further help?"

"I refuse to let you command this post, sir!"

Gedso looked uncomfortable and unhappy. He finally turned to the door and laid his hand on the knob. He was trying to think of something further to say, but failed. The door stuck and came off its shattered hinges before he could lessen the slight jerk he had given it. Amid the ruins of glass he looked apologetically at the apoplectic general.

Stewie got up from the orderly bench. "Did he refuse?"

"Yes," said Gedso.

"You got any further ideas?" said Stewie.

"I can appeal to my superiors—but they dislike technicians who have to resort to them."

"Well," said Stewie, wrinkling up his stub of a nose, "all I can say is that one way or the other I'll get it. I never did like those acid baths they use. How bad do you want to go on past the mines?"

"Unless we do, there won't be any mines within the year."

"And there won't be any Stewie in two days. Didn't you show him any facts? I couldn't make anything of anything, of course, but he ought to be able to figure out what you're adding up."

"He wouldn't look at my data. These military men can think only in terms of weapons and he has been angry from the first because he thought I came here to devise something better than the arc cannon and then wouldn't do my job. He says I'm stalling."

"Uh-uh," said Stewie with a thoughtfully half-closed eye upon a cargo ship which was landing. The ship was disgorging new tanks of the latest pattern. Soldiers were rolling them into line and, as fast as they were started up, were driving them toward the shops. Stewie grinned.

Gedso followed Stewie's gaze and then understood. Together they walked toward the ramp down which the tanks were being disgorged from the ship.

"Are they what you want?" said Stewie.

"They will do very well," said Gedso.

Stewie took a position at the bottom of the ramp and the next tank which came down stopped rolling just beside him. He climbed quickly to the turret and in an officious voice began to give directions for its alignment in the column. Caring very little, the convicts pushed.

Gedso climbed through the portway and, glancing over the rocket turbine, threw the fuel feeds and switches on. Stewie dropped down and into the driver's seat and touched the throttles, letting the tank creep forward. At the machine and fuel shops, Stewie paused beside the crystal chutes and the automatic loaders crammed the storage compartment full. At the armament shed a bundle of electric cartridges rattled into the magazine.

Then a footfall sounded upon the slope of the metal giant and the hatch was jerked open. A pair of officers' ironplast boots dropped into sight and a familiar face was thrust, with startled expression, in Gedso's. And before a word had passed, General Drummond, inspecting new equipment as a good officer should, dropped down beside his trusty Blufore. Drummond was not as quick in sensing the situation.

"Very good, very good. Perhaps they appreciate us just a little after all, eh, Cascot? These seem well built and well armed. Far too comfortable, though, for their cre— Saints!"

Blufore had been trying to say something for seconds, but he had an abnormally strong hand over his mouth.

Drummond was thrust into a seat by Gedso's other hand and the hatch above slammed shut, leaving the place lighted only by the sparks which escaped the rocket turbines.

"What is this?" cried Drummond.

"I don't know," said Gedso, "of two officers who could be of more help. I hope you won't mind. I'm sorry, in fact. But the Scienticorps appropriated and commandeered this tank before it was receipted into your command. Therefore it is technically my command. I am sorry, but we have too much to do to be stopped. Please, pardon us."

"Let us out of here this instant!" brayed Drummond. "I'll have my guards tear you to bits! I'll have your card! I'll get you a court martial that they'll talk about for years. This is kidnapping!"

"This is necessity," said Gedso. "I am sorry. Drive Stewie."

An astonished patrol on the outer wall gazed upon the spectacle of a charging tank which swiftly burned its way through the spun silica and raced into the rocky distance to be lost in the immensity where no tank or ship or division had ever ventured before.

At the far end of the vaulted chamber, Technician Brown, deaf to the violent stream of objection which stormed about him, consulted a chart of his own drawing, a cartographic masterpiece which read in three dimensions having been constructed out of descriptive geometry.

"Ahead, over that hump," said Gedso, "there should be another tunnel, probably not more than two kilometers wide. You will need much power for the going will be very rough and the grade very steep."

"Aye, aye," said Stewie. "Why don't you bat those guys one and make 'em shut up?"

This speech from a convict gunner was entirely too much for General Drummond. His eyes dilated and his nostrils flared like those of a battle horse of Gerlon about to charge. Thus, Stewie had the desired quiet long enough to get the tank through a particularly rough area and climb the indicated hump.

There ahead was the passage which Gedso had predicted and Stewie spent a little breath in admiration. "Gee, how'd you know that that was going to turn up right there? You act like you'd been here before."

"No man has ever been here before," mourned Blufore, a-wallow in self-pity, "and no man will ever be again."

Drummond was given much satisfaction as soon as they started down into the mouth of the ascending tunnel, for in a space of instants, a weaving mass threw itself in their way. The "things" choked the channel and then swept back along its sides until both the advance and the retreat of the tank were covered. It was impossible to clearly make out their maneuvers or numbers, for one received only an impression of vague hugeness on the march as though mountains were moving.

Stewie looked alertly at Gedso for orders.

"Transfer gravity," said Gedso. "Perhaps they won't be able to rush across above for a moment!"

A new whining note cried through the ship and the gymbals in which the control room was suspended creaked as they allowed the room to invert. With a crunch the tank struck against the upper side of the tunnel and, scrambling

183

for traction, began to run there. Below the moving horde flowed ominously along, joined every moment by additional thousands.

"You'll never make it," said Drummond. "This crackpot craving to explore will cost all of us our lives." He seemed to find much gratification in the fact.

"Please," pleaded Stewie, "can't we jettison that Jonah?"

"There's a fork of the tunnel just ahead," said Gedso, studying his chart. "We go to the right."

"Right or left," said Drummond, "you'll never make it, you clumsy lout!" He got up. "I order you to return instantly. If you do not obey, I'll . . . I'll have you shot!"

"Please," said Stewie, "can't I spring that under hatch and let him out?"

"We turn into the main tunnel here," said Gedso, pointing.

They entered a cavernous place, larger than the mines, larger than any interior so far seen. The weirdly glowing walls curved down to a crystal-strewn floor forty-three kilometers below them. Moving on the debris were the legions of "things," augmented in number until they congested the tunnel.

"Thank Jala they don't fly," said Stewie. "How much farther do we have to go?"

"About seventy kilometers," said Gedso.

"And then what do we do?"

"Then we'll probably run into the main body of the 'things'."

Stewie frowned for a short time, trying to figure out if Technician Brown meant to attack

184

the main army with one flimsy tank. But thought was irksome to Stewie over a certain duration and he lost himself in the management of the tank.

After a little, the passage ahead became blocked, at least so far as Stewie could tell.

"Keep going," said Gedso. "There may be a narrow space at the top. That stuff up ahead will be moving and so don't lose control."

Approaching closer, the movement was perceptible, resembling a slow-motion avalanche. Reaching the upper rim and perceiving an opening, Stewie tried to make the tank climb straight up. But the traction was bad and with a lurch it fell backward to strike heavily upon the rocky slide. It spun on one track, fell over and, with racing turbines, clawed upward over the treacherous ground. Drummond dabbed at a cut on his forehead and glared in a promising way at Stewie's back.

At the top they found themselves in close confines and had to pick their way through passes in the rock. They traveled several kilometers before they could again find clear travel and then only by using a step wall as their roadway.

The "things" had been left behind for some little time, but now they came upon an isolated beast which scuttled down at them like a mountainous spider.

Stewie pressed the electrode triggers and the arc licked thunderously out to lock through the body. The "thing" closed over the tank, engulfing it and tearing it away from the wall. A gigantic maw was opened and they were sucked into it on the rush of air which, hurri-canelike, spun them and toppled them down.

Gedso flashed on their flood lamps and the interior of the "thing" showed about them in dirty confusion. The tank settled to its gravity side and the tracks churned in the soggy morass.

With a swift change of fuel feeds, Gedso brought the reactionary tubes into play and the tank slammed itself against the inside wall which indented and then snapped back into place, hurling them across to the far side.

"Hold on and try it again," said Gedso.

This time the reactionary blast let them gather momentum. There was a roaring sound as the inner lining of the "thing" ripped. The sides of the wound clamped down and held the tank fast. Stewie shortened the arc to minimum range and played it full blast upon the outside scale wall. Smoke obscured their vision.

"Try her traction now," said Gedso.

The turbine sparked and spewed out ozone. Slowly and then with a charging rush, the tank blasted through. Stewie steered for the high wall without a backward glance at the death agonies of the "thing."

Drummond was shaking and glassy-eyed, but he held to his nerve. "If you've learned enough," he said with acid-dripping words, "perhaps you might make it back."

"Too many waiting for us back there now," said Gedso. "There are smaller tunnels they can block completely."

"Then what do you mean to do?" flared Drummond.

"Up this incline and through that slit," said Gedso to Stewie.

The tank scrambled up the wall and darted through.

It was as though they had come upon a conclave of the "things." Or an ambush. The place was packed with them and the walls were less than a thousand meters apart and not eighty meters high.

"Up!" said Gedso. "Reverse your gravity!" And then, "Hold on at the top here."

Below the "things" had awakened to the presence of the interloper and now began to tumble over one another and climb on backs to strike at the object above them. Other "things" poured into the cavern and, by sheer volume, the height steadily decreased.

Gedso was staring anxiously around the interior of the place into which they had come. Here the walls were not flat, but arranged in a regular pattern of hummocks. And at the end was one particular knoll, much bigger than the rest. The range to it was about two hundred and twenty meters.

With powerful hands Gedso poised the arc cannon and let drive at the hummock. The green-yellow streak lit up the crawling scene below.

"Advance on that target," said Gedso.

Stewie eased the tank forward, trying not to look at the thickening multitude which was coming up to them. Smoke was flying from the hummock and the top of it was becoming charred. As they approached they could see that it was a nub of something which, in gigantic volume, reached out beyond. The arc cannon ate steadily into it, biting off dozens of cubic meters a second, for the stuff appeared to be very soft and highly inflammable.

A feeler was touching the tank now and then, with decreasing intervals and increasing force.

The arc cannon had started the hummock burning and now it began to char under its own combustion, disappearing in smoke in cubic kilometers. Then the smoke volume was so great that not even the arc was visible in it.

A heavy blow against the tank knocked it loose. It was knocked about with swift ferocity in the sea of angry "things" until a maw spread apart and dashed them in.

They tumbled down a passage much larger than that of the "thing" which had taken them before and a bony structure, visible to their floodlights, reacted upon three of the occupants of the tank like steel bars upon a prisoner.

Finally, bruised and shaken, they came to rest, half sunk in mire.

With a final sob of despair, Blufore hid his head in his hands and cried. Drummond looked steadily at Gedso.

With a shrug, Stewie said, "Well, we sure gave them a hell of a time while we lasted. There's enough air in the containers for maybe a day and after that—well, maybe he can digest armor plate."

Gedso sat down in the engineer's seat and stretched out his legs. He took an apple out of his pocket, polished it upon his sleeve and took a soul-satisfying bite. "I wouldn't worry too much," he said, glancing at his watch. "We'll probably be out of here before that day is up."

"A lot of good that will do," said Drummond. "We'll *never* get back."

Gedso finished his apple and then composed himself. In a little while he was asleep.

Some time later, at Gedso's order, the tank moved slowly up the way it had come and, much to everyone's—save Gedso's—surprise, there was no resistance to their return through the maw which gaped stiffly and made no effort to close even when they churned out over the lower jaw.

Although some smoke remained in the small cavern, only charred ruin marked where the hummock had been. And there were no "things" to bar their way, only sodden lumps strewn about in stiff attitudes.

Stewie guided them along the return route, but nowhere did they find anything alive. The contrast of this with their recent difficulties made even Drummond forget his quarrel, and Blufore gazed hopefully about.

"What's the meaning of this?" demanded Drummond, pointing out yet another vast pile of motionless "things" which lay open-mouthed in a tunnel, not even moving when run over by the tank.

"That's the way things are," said Gedso indifferently.

"I . . . I'd like to *know* how they are," said Drummond.

"You'll probably get a copy of my report," said Gedso. "To the left here, Stewie."

"I probably won't get that for a long time," said Drummond, pouting. "I ought to know so as to regulate the activities in my command." He looked pleadingly at Gedso. "What did going 'outside' have to do with this?"

"Had to find out about the Black Nebula," said Gedso matter-of-factly. "Right, Stewie. Right and down."

"Well, damn it, what about the Black Nebula?"

Gedso turned toward him patiently in surrender. "The Black Nebula isn't a barrier in the sky. I'm not sure what it is. A fold, perhaps. I don't know. I had to get pictures of this area from out there." He reached into his pocket and brought out a photomontage. "Reduced the pictures after they were taken with an inverted telephoto. Got this."

"Why, that looks like a leaf," said Drummond. "And what is that on the leaf?"

"A leaf," said Gedso, "and on the leaf, to you, a caterpillar worm."

"You mean th?s is a picture of the 'outside'?"

"Yes. The Crystal Mines are in the liver of that worm and the crystals are so valuable because they are, of course, highly condensed cellular energy."

Drummond was round-eyed with awe. "Then . . . then I am the outpost command of a world beyond the Black Nebula, a world so gigantic that even a worm is thousands of kilometers long!"

"When I inspected the Black Nebula," said Gedso gently, "I discovered that it was not a barrier in space, but a fold or some such thing.

As I say, I don't know. I only know the effect. Ships approaching the Crystal Mines undergo a sort of transformation. The reason so many never return is because they fail to reverse that transformation and so hurtle through the hundreds of light-years forever, no larger than microscopic bullets."

"What's that?"

"Well, according to what we found, a diminution of size takes place. The worm is just an ordinary worm on an ordinary leaf. And the 'things' are just ordinary phagocytes. If we proceed in the future to burn out the heart of the worms we mine, then we will have to do no fighting. Because of a changed time factor a dead worm will last for years. And if we watch certain manifestations in the space ships, we can get them to keep penetrating the Black Nebula until they are again restored to size. I took a chart of the interior of these worms out of a text on entymology, once I had determined the kind of worm it was—"

"Then . . . then my command—"

"Why, yes," said Gedso, "I think it is so. You need have no worries about your command. No more fighting, better conditions, more crystals mined—"

"But," gagged Drummond, deflated and broken, "but my command . . . is just the liver of an ordinary worm . . . perhaps in a tree in some farmer's yard—"

Stewie grinned as he steered across the plane to the wall of the Crystal Mines. He took another glance at the haggard General Dummond and pulled up at the wall.

When fifty thousand convicts, the following day, cheered themselves to a frenzy carrying Gedso Ion Brown, Technician, Extra-Territorial Scienticorps, to his waiting transport, General Drummond was not there. In the dimness of his quarters, amid his presentation pistols and battle trophies, he heard the racking waves of triumphant sound sweep the mines again and again for minutes at a time.

General Drummond sank into a chair and cupped his face in his hands.

Wearily he repeated, "The guts . . . of a worm."